Welcome to this month's books from Harlequin
Presents! The fabulously passionate series
THE ROYAL HOUSE OF NIROLI continues with
The Tycoon's Princess Bride by Natasha Oakley,
where Princess Isabella Fierezza risks forfeiting
her chance to be queen when she falls for
Niroli's enemy, Domenic Vincini. And don't miss
The Spanish Prince's Virgin Bride, the final part of
Sandra Marton's trilogy THE BILLIONAIRES' BRIDES, in
which Prince Lucas Reyes believes his contract fiancée
is pretending she's never been touched by another man!

Also this month, favorite author Helen Bianchin brings
you *The Greek Tycoon's Virgin Wife,* where gorgeous
Xandro Caramanis wants a wife—and an heir. In
Innocent on Her Wedding Night by Sara Craven,
Daniel meets his estranged wife again—and wants
to claim the wedding night that was never his. In
The Boss's Wife for a Week by Anne McAllister,
Spence Tyack's assistant Sadie proves not only to be
sensible in the boardroom, but also sensual in the
bedroom! In *The Mediterranean Billionaire's Secret
Baby* by Diana Hamilton, Italian billionaire Francesco
Mastroianni is shocked to see his ex-mistress again after
seven months—and she's visibly pregnant! In *Willingly
Bedded, Forcibly Wedded* by Melanie Milburne,
Jasper Caulfield has to marry Hayley or he'll lose his
inheritance. But she's determined to be a wife on paper
only. Finally brilliant new author India Grey brings you
her first book, *The Italian's Defiant Mistress,* where
only millionaire Raphael di Lazaro can help Eve—if she
becomes his mistress....

Bedded by...

Blackmail

Forced to bed...then to wed?

He's got her firmly in his sights and she's got only one chance of survival—surrender to his blackmail...and him...in his bed!

Bedded by... **Blackmail**

The *big* miniseries from Harlequin Presents®...

Dare you read it?

Melanie Milburne

WILLINGLY BEDDED, FORCIBLY WEDDED

Bedded by...

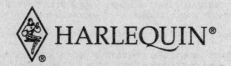

Forced to bed...then to wed?

HARLEQUIN®

TORONTO • NEW YORK • LONDON
AMSTERDAM • PARIS • SYDNEY • HAMBURG
STOCKHOLM • ATHENS • TOKYO • MILAN • MADRID
PRAGUE • WARSAW • BUDAPEST • AUCKLAND

If you purchased this book without a cover you should be aware that this book is stolen property. It was reported as "unsold and destroyed" to the publisher, and neither the author nor the publisher has received any payment for this "stripped book."

ISBN-13: 978-0-373-12673-6
ISBN-10:   0-373-12673-5

WILLINGLY BEDDED, FORCIBLY WEDDED

First North American Publication 2007.

Copyright © 2007 by Melanie Milburne.

All rights reserved. Except for use in any review, the reproduction or utilization of this work in whole or in part in any form by any electronic, mechanical or other means, now known or hereafter invented, including xerography, photocopying and recording, or in any information storage or retrieval system, is forbidden without the written permission of the publisher, Harlequin Enterprises Limited, 225 Duncan Mill Road, Don Mills, Ontario, Canada M3B 3K9.

This is a work of fiction. Names, characters, places and incidents are either the product of the author's imagination or are used fictitiously, and any resemblance to actual persons, living or dead, business establishments, events or locales is entirely coincidental.

This edition published by arrangement with Harlequin Books S.A.

® and TM are trademarks of the publisher. Trademarks indicated with ® are registered in the United States Patent and Trademark Office, the Canadian Trade Marks Office and in other countries.

www.eHarlequin.com

Printed in U.S.A.

All about the author...
Melanie Milburne

MELANIE MILBURNE read her first Harlequin novel when she was seventeen and has never looked back. She decided she would settle for nothing less than a tall, dark and handsome hero as her future husband. Well, not only is she still reading romance, she's writing it, as well! And the tall, dark and handsome hero? She fell in love with him on the second date and was secretly engaged to him within six weeks!

Two sons later they arrived in Hobart, Tasmania—the jewel in the Australian crown. Once their boys were in school, Melanie went back to university and received her bachelor's and master's degrees.

For her final assessment she conducted a tutorial in literary theory concentrating on the romance genre. As she was reading a paragraph from the novel of a prominent Harlequin author, the door suddenly burst open. The husband she thought was working was actually standing there, dressed in a tuxedo, his dark brown eyes centered on her startled blue ones. He strode across the room, hauled Melanie into his arms and kissed her deeply and passionately before setting her back down and leaving without a single word. The lecturer gave Melanie a high distinction and her fellow students gave her jealous glares! And so her pilgrimage into romance writing was set!

Melanie also enjoys long-distance running and is a nationally ranked top-ten masters swimmer in Australia. She learned to swim as an adult, so for anyone who thinks they can't do something—you can! Her motto is "Don't say I can't. Say I CAN TRY."

To Jan Heyward-Casey

There can be no more beautiful person working in the beauty industry than you. Thank you for all your love and support and for waxing my worries away both literally and figuratively! Love you heaps.

CHAPTER ONE

'*MARRIED?*' JASPER CAULFIELD almost choked on the word. 'Are you out of your cotton-picking mind?'

Duncan Brocklehurst gave his client an empathetic look. 'I guess it's your father's way of still exerting control from the other side of the grave.'

Jasper's dark brows snapped together irritably. 'You mean there's no way out of it?'

The lawyer shook his head. 'I'm afraid not, Jasper. If you want the Crickglades estate you're going to have to fulfil the terms of the old man's will, and soon, otherwise the whole lot is going to your brother Raymond.'

Jasper sprang to his feet and began to pace the room in agitation. 'This is totally outrageous. Raymond's a priest for God's sake. What's he going to do with a place the size of Crickglades?'

'Look, it might not be so bad,' Duncan consoled him. 'All you have to do is convince Hayley Addington to be your wife and live with her for a month and the place is yours.'

Jasper turned around to glare at him. 'Hayley Addington? Are you completely nuts? Even if I was the marrying type, which I'm very definitely not, she's practically the last woman I would consider tying myself to, even temporarily. Besides, she hates my guts.'

'Which is probably why Gerald constructed his will this way,' Duncan pointed out. 'But for all that it does seem a rather strange caveat.'

'Strange?' Jasper gave an incredulous snort. 'It's bloody ridiculous, that's what it is. Who on earth gets married for a month?'

'I know it's unusual but I'd think about it very seriously if I were you,' Duncan said. 'This is a property developer's dream. The land is worth a fortune in terms of redevelopment. Surely it's worth putting up with a short term marriage?'

Jasper blew out a breath as he sat back down. He had his own reasons for wanting Crickglades—and he was damned well going to make sure he got what he wanted. He scraped a hand through his thick black hair before fixing his gaze on the document on the desk as if it were something poisonous. 'So how am I going to convince Hayley to marry me?'

Duncan chuckled with amusement. 'You are *such* a comedian.' He leaned back in his chair, still grinning. 'Why not use some of that lethal charm you're so well known for? You have a veritable drove of adoring women following you about all the time if what's reported in the press is to be believed.'

Jasper rolled his eyes. 'Yeah, well, it's going to take a lot more than charm to get Hayley to agree with this. Anyway, what does she get out of the deal? I was under the impression she'd sweet talked him into leaving her the lot. Did the old guy change his mind at the last minute?'

'His previous will had been pretty straightforward but he drew up a new one a few days before he died.' Duncan's eyes flicked back to the legal papers in front of him. 'This time around she gets a lump sum from Gerald's estate, but only if she marries you and lives with you for the month as stated.'

'How much is the lump sum?'

Duncan told him an amount that made Jasper's dark brows shoot upwards. 'That much, huh?'

'Yep,' Duncan said. 'A nice little carrot, if you ask me.'

Jasper's expression twisted cynically. 'It wouldn't matter what size carrot my father had organised, she'd never agree to marry me,' he said, his frown deepening. 'What was the old man thinking of?'

'I don't know, but your father insisted no money must change hands between you. You can't pay Hayley to be your wife. And no pre-nup either.'

Jasper jerked upright in his chair. *'What?'*

Duncan pushed the document across the desk for him to inspect the fine print. 'There it is in black and white. No pre-nuptial agreement.'

'That's just financial suicide!' Jasper raged. 'This is total madness, especially when you consider what happened to my father when Hayley's bitch of a mother Eva stripped him of half his assets. Come on, surely there's a way around this?'

Duncan shook his head. 'Sorry, Jasper. Your father has tied this up so neatly it would take more than Houdini to get out of it. You really have no choice but to do as it says. Get Hayley Addington to be your wife, then hope and pray she doesn't still hate you at the end of the month and take you to the cleaners.'

Jasper rubbed at his jaw for a moment. 'Does she know the details of the will?'

'I met with her yesterday.'

'And?'

Duncan gave him a sober look. 'You've got yourself one hell of a challenge on your hands, Jasper,' he said. 'Not only does she hate you to hell and back, she's currently engaged to another man.'

Jasper felt as if someone had punched him in the midsection. *'Engaged?'*

Duncan nodded. 'You'll have to work quickly as she plans to get married some time next month.'

Jasper's one short, sharp curse cut the air like a knife.

Hayley engaged? How did that happen without him finding out about it? Not that it was any of his business, of course, but then again…

'She mentioned to me you hadn't gone to the funeral,' Duncan interrupted Jasper's wandering thoughts.

His eyes moved away from the lawyer's to look at the array of graduation certificates on the wall. 'I didn't make it back in time,' he said in a flat emotionless tone, which he hoped belied the truth of what he was feeling. 'I was overseas on business.'

'She wasn't too happy about it, I might add,' Duncan went on. 'She was under the impression you were cavorting in the Caribbean with Collette or Claudia or whatever your current girlfriend's name is.'

Jasper turned back to look at him. 'Her name is Candice and she's no longer current.'

'Just as well, then,' Duncan said in a pragmatic tone. 'So when was the last time you saw Hayley?'

'A few years ago at one of my father's fund-raising garden parties for Raymond's parish, I think,' he said, inwardly wincing as the memory returned. 'I made some comment about the outfit she was wearing and she threw her drink in my face. It ruined a brand-new designer shirt, I might add.'

'Charming.'

'Yeah, that's Hayley, all right,' Jasper said with a curl of his lip. 'But it's a pity my father couldn't see what a little cat she was. You'd have thought he would have learned from his experience with her sluttish mother, but no—he thought Hayley was different. He thought the sun shone out of her blue-green eyes. God, it used to make me sick the way she sucked up to him all the time.'

'You never know, she might have changed for the better,' Duncan said. 'She seemed all right to me when I met her yesterday. I thought she was rather sweet, actually.'

Jasper grunted. 'You spent an hour with her. I supposedly have to spend a bloody month with her.'

'That's if you can convince her to marry you instead of Myles Lederman,' Duncan reminded him.

'Myles Lederman, eh?' Jasper rubbed his chin thoughtfully. 'My brother Raymond is right,' he said with a glinting smile. 'There must be a god after all.'

'You know this Lederman fellow?' Duncan asked.

'We've crossed paths a couple of times.'

'Yes, well, I still think you've got a bit of a fight on your hands even if you do have some convenient connections,' Duncan said.

Jasper got to his feet and gave the lawyer a determined look as he reached for the door. 'If I have to drag Hayley kicking and screaming to the altar I'll damn well do it. You just watch me.'

'Your next client is here,' Lucy informed Hayley as she poked her head around the facial room door.

'Thanks, Lucy,' Hayley said as she straightened the covers on the treatment table. 'I'll be out in a second to get her.'

'Erm…' Lucy cleared her throat. 'It's not a her—it's a him. A rather gorgeous him too, I might add.'

Hayley turned around with a frown. 'But Mrs Fairbright always comes in at this time for her eyebrow tint. Did she cancel at the last minute?'

'Must have,' Lucy said. 'Anyway I'm sure you won't be disappointed in her replacement. God, I wish I could wax his chest or whatever it is he wants done.'

'What *does* he want done?'

Lucy shrugged. 'I don't know. I didn't look at the appointment book. He just said he had an appointment at three p.m. with you. He was quite adamant about it, actually.'

'Then if I'm the one he wants, then that's who he's going to get,' Hayley said with pride, and began quoting her brand new mission statement. 'That's what Bayside Best for Beauty is all about: giving our clients, both male and female, a truly memorable beauty therapy experience.'

She smoothed down her smart pink and white uniform and pasted a bright smile on her face as she went out to Reception, only to come up short when a tall figure unfolded himself from one of the suede-covered chairs.

'*You!*' she gasped in shock.

'Nice to see you too, Hayley,' Jasper drawled. 'How's tricks?'

She clenched her teeth and stamped her foot. 'Get out of my salon. *Now.*'

He rocked back on his heels in an indolent manner as he looked around the plush reception area of the salon. 'Your salon, huh?' He whistled through his teeth and brought his dark brown eyes back to her flashing blue-green ones. 'What a pity you won't be able to keep it.'

She looked at him through narrowed eyes. 'What did you say?'

He smiled one of his lazy smiles. 'I've just purchased some real estate on this block. It was an absolute bargain. A steal, you could say.'

She felt a sudden chugging in her chest as if her heart were trying to decide whether to beat harder or stop altogether. 'So?'

'So…' he said, deliberately pausing over the word, 'as of today I am your new landlord.'

Hayley gaped at him. 'But…but that's impossible!'

He folded his arms across his broad chest, his dark gaze gleaming with satisfaction. 'The legal work was finalised this morning,' he said. 'That's why I am here.'

The front door pinged cheerily as another client came in. Hayley gave the woman a quick smile of greeting and mumbled something about Lucy attending to her shortly, before she turned back to Jasper. 'We can't discuss this out here,' she said in a stiff undertone. 'You'd better come to my office out the back.'

She led the way on leaden legs, her stomach feeling as if someone were twisting her insides into hard little knots. Every time she saw Jasper Caulfield she felt anger charging through her system like high voltage electricity. She hadn't seen him in three years and yet nothing had changed.

She still hated him with a vengeance.

She pushed open her office door and took refuge behind her desk, but it wasn't much of a barrier. As soon as he came in the room it seemed to shrink to half its size, and when he took the chair opposite she felt the brush of his long legs against hers under the desk. She clamped her thighs together and hastily repositioned her legs as she sent him another gimlet glare.

'I suppose you're going to charge me an outrageous rent or something,' she bit out resentfully.

'That depends,' he said, his dark inscrutable eyes running over her taut features.

'On what?'

'Your cooperation.'

She grasped the edge of the desk with both hands. 'Why don't you get straight to the point?' she asked. 'If you're here to try and intimidate me, then you can leave right now. It won't work.'

'Actually I'm here on another matter.'

'Oh?' She gave him a scornful look. 'So you want a deluxe facial after all, do you?'

'I want you to be my wife.'

Hayley blinked at him. 'Your *what*?'

'I want you to marry me,' he said, his darker-than-night gaze still holding hers.

'You have *got* to be joking.'

'I'm not.'

She got to her feet and slammed her chair back into the desk. 'How dare you come here and waste my time?' she railed at him. 'I know it's a hackneyed cliché, but I told Gerald's lawyer yesterday I wouldn't marry you if you were the last man on earth and you damn well know it.'

'Don't tell me I have to eradicate every other man on earth to see if you're really telling the truth,' he remarked dryly.

She blew out a furious breath and pointed to the door with a rigid arm. 'Get out!'

He leaned back in his chair and crossed one ankle over his knee, his casual pose infuriating her even further.

'Make me,' he said.

Hayley felt a fluttery sensation in the pit of her stomach at the glinting challenge in his eyes. Her heart began to thump erratically and her legs were quivering and shaking as if they had just run a marathon without the benefit of training. Being in Jasper Caulfield's presence always had that effect on her. She didn't understand how someone she hated so much could make her feel so angry and yet so nervous and unsure of herself at the same time.

'I'm going to ask you one more time to leave and then I'm going to call the police,' she said, trying to make her voice sound firm.

He got to his feet and came to stand right in front of her. She took a step backwards but her office was too small for it to make much difference.

'G-get away from me,' she said with an edge of desperation in her voice.

He took another step, his eyes locking on hers. 'What are you frightened of, Hayley?' he asked. 'That I might kiss you like you begged me to all those years ago?'

She clenched her teeth, her face flaming with remembered shame of her one lapse of self-control. 'You wouldn't dare.'

'Oh, I dare all right,' he said smoothly, reaching out to capture a lock of her dark curly hair and slowly coiling it around his finger.

Hayley swallowed as the hairs on her scalp responded to the tether of his touch, her stomach folding over itself as his chest moved close enough to brush against her breasts. She was deeply ashamed of how her body responded to the closeness of his. She could feel the subtle tightening of her nipples against the lace of her bra, her body weakening as a silky ribbon of traitorous desire began to unfurl deep inside her.

'Aren't you f-forgetting something?' she asked somewhat breathlessly. 'I'm already engaged to be married.'

'Call it off.'

'No, I will not call it off!'

'He's having an affair, you know,' he said.

'That's a slanderous lie!'

'I have proof.'

'I don't believe you,' she said, but the niggling doubts she had been pushing away for the last few days began to nudge her yet again.

'I have photos if you want to see them,' he said into the silence. 'Her name is Serena Wiltshire. Tall, leggy blonde, big boobs and a killer smile.'

Hayley felt a wave of nausea flow over her. How could Myles have done this to her? They were getting married next month. She'd just paid for the honeymoon during her lunch break. He'd told her he loved her. He was the first man in fact who had ever done so. He had promised her the world, marriage and babies and a house in a harbourside suburb.

Security.

And she loved him…

Of course she loved him; she shoved the creeping doubt back beneath the bolted door inside her head.

'So how about it, Hayley?' Jasper said, his breath whispering over the surface of her lips. 'Do you fancy being my wife for a month?'

'I can't think of anything worse,' she scratched out.

His dark eyes twinkled. 'I don't know about that,' he said. 'What if I took your salon away from you? Wouldn't that be far worse?'

'You wouldn't d—'

He blocked the rest of her sentence with the warm pad of his index finger on the soft cushion of her lips. 'Oh, I dare all right,' he repeated his previous words with chilling determination. 'You just watch me, sweetheart.'

Hayley gulped back her rising panic. She was only just managing to meet the rent now; how much worse would it be if he decided to charge her an exorbitant sum? The business loan she'd taken out recently for the refurbishment of the salon had stretched her to the limit, and, although the salon was doing well, any extra financial pressure right now would be nothing short of disastrous.

'When you think about it, Hayley, this is a perfect chance for you to get revenge on your cheating fiancé,' he said, dropping his hand from her mouth. 'Tell Lederman you've fallen in love with me. It will really get to him that you've chosen me over him.'

'No one would ever believe me if I told them I was in love with you,' she said, injecting her tone with scorn even as her lips continued to buzz with the sensation of his touch. 'They'll think I was marrying you for your money.'

'I guess we'll both have to brush up on our acting skills,' he returned. 'You're not exactly the woman of my dreams either. I wouldn't go as far as saying you're the last woman on the earth and all that, but you're way down on that list somewhere.'

She glared up at him. 'I see you failed the entrance exam to charm school again.'

He laughed and stepped back from her, the deep rich sound sending a shock wave of reaction through her stomach.

She watched as he wandered over to her desk and picked up a recent photo of his father she had taken a few days before he died. He stood looking down at it for a long time before he put it back on the desk, his expression when he turned to face her once more devoid of emotion.

'I'll give you a call in a couple of days,' he said. 'In the meantime don't do anything I wouldn't do.'

She gave a cynical little grunt. 'That certainly leaves the field wild open. It seems to me there's very little you wouldn't do to get your own way.'

He blew her a kiss across the flat of his extended palm. 'Love you too, Hayley.'

Hayley felt a tiny shiver of apprehension run up her spine as the door closed on his exit. There was something about Jasper Caulfield that had always signalled danger. She had never felt entirely safe around him in all the years she'd known him.

Marrying him was out of the question.

She wasn't even going to think about it.

No way.

Not even for a minute.

She didn't dare…

CHAPTER TWO

'ARE WE STILL on for dinner tonight, Myles?' Hayley asked, holding the phone to her ear as she checked her make-up in the mirror above her bathroom basin of her small inner-city rented flat.

'Er…tonight might be a bit of a problem, my dear,' Myles said. 'I've got a new client I have to see. It was a last-minute booking. I can't really get out of it. Sorry.'

Hayley turned her back on the flash of pain and disappointment she could see in her blue-green gaze. This was the third night in a row Myles had cancelled their arrangements.

'That's OK,' she said, trying not to sound too let down. 'I have some paperwork to see to anyway.'

'Sorry about that, Hayley. I'll give you a call tomorrow. Maybe we can get together then.'

'Fine,' she said. 'Hope it goes well with your client tonight.'

'Yes…yes, I'm sure it will. Bye.'

Hayley had only just ended the call when the phone rang again in her hand. She didn't recognise the caller ID number but answered it anyway. 'Hello, Hayley Addington speaking.'

'So you *are* still speaking to me, then,' Jasper commented wryly.

Her hands tightened on the receiver. 'Get off my phone.'

'Have dinner with me?' he asked, totally unfazed by her acid tone.

'You must be joking.'

'I know this great place we can go,' he said. 'It's really swanky. You never know who you might see there.'

'I'm busy tonight,' she said through tight lips.

'No,' he said. 'You're going to sit at home all by your little lonesome self, missing your fiancé who just cancelled your dinner date for the third time this week, right?'

She gripped the phone even tighter. 'How on earth do you know that? Have you got a tap on my phone or something?'

His deep chuckle lifted the fine hairs on the back of her neck. 'Come on, sweetheart,' he said. 'I need you and you need me. Let's go and have dinner and if we happen to run into your cheating fiancé you can tell him to his face that you've changed your mind about marrying him.'

'Myles is having dinner with a client,' she said, doing her best to ignore those niggling little doubts again. 'He's a busy real estate agent with a lot of high-profile clients. Entertaining them is one of the demands of the job.'

'If that's the case, then you should have no concerns about coming with me to dinner at the same restaurant,' he pointed out. 'If Myles's dinner is all above board he'll just assume we're having dinner together like any other stepbrother and stepsister.'

'We are *not* stepbrother and sister,' she protested hotly, 'or at least not any more.'

'How is your mother, by the way?' he asked. 'What number husband is she on to now? Is it four or five?'

Six, actually, Hayley was tempted to say, but didn't, knowing it would only make things worse. She hadn't seen her mother in months but there was no way she was going to tell him that. 'You are *such* a jerk,' she said instead.

'I'll be around in twenty minutes to pick you up.'

'Don't you dare!'

He chuckled again. 'Don't dare me, sweetheart. You know how much it gets me all worked up.'

'I won't go out with you!' she shrieked at him. 'I won't!'

He didn't answer. She wanted to throw the phone at nearest wall, but she stopped herself just in time.

But only just.

She snatched up her car keys instead and bolted out the door.

The popular new harbourside restaurant was crowded but Hayley saw Myles as soon as she came in. He was sitting at one of the tables at the back, his hands holding those of a buxom blonde woman who was looking adoringly into his eyes. He was smiling as if he had just won the lottery, his round cheeks flushed with pleasure as he leaned forward across the table to plant a smacking kiss to the woman's pouting scarlet-painted lips.

Hayley was so shocked she didn't register at first that someone had come in the door behind her. She felt a solid warm presence at her back and, turning, looked a long way upwards into the dark, fathomless depths of Jasper Caulfield's gaze.

'Hey, baby girl,' he said softly as he reached for her hand, his larger one totally swallowing hers. 'Let's get it over with. I booked the spot three tables from theirs.'

Hayley felt her legs following him even though everything else in her screamed to get out and get out now. She gulped back her anguish as Myles swivelled his head sideways, his eyes widening in shock and a good measure of shame as she and Jasper came to a standstill in front of them.

'Hayley…' Myles choked, his face flushing a deep beetroot. 'W-what are you doing here?'

'I…I…'

Jasper squeezed her hand in encouragement.

'Myles…I've come to a decision,' she said, briefly tightening her fingers around Jasper's. 'I—I want to end our engagement.'

Myles's eyes nearly popped out of his head. 'You can't mean that!'

'She does,' Jasper said firmly. 'She's marrying me instead.'

'You must be joking!' Myles said, his throat moving up and down like a piston.

'It's over, Myles,' Hayley said, handing back her engagement ring, feeling as if she was handing back her chance for a secure, predictable future as well.

Myles's jaw dropped. 'But you have to marry me! You have to!'

'Why?' Jasper asked before Hayley could speak.

'Because…' His Adam's apple bobbed up and down again. 'Because you love me…you do, don't you, Hayley?'

'Actually I don't,' Hayley said, biting her lip for a moment. 'I thought I did but…but all this time I've been secretly in love with Jasper.'

'*Jasper?*' Myles's jaw dropped. 'But you've always said how much you hated him. How he made your teenage years miserable and—'

'That's all sorted out now,' Hayley inserted hastily, determined to walk away from Myles with at least some of her pride intact. 'We've fallen in love and are getting married as soon as possible.'

'But what about the wedding arrangements?' he said. 'My mother has invited so many people. I've paid a fortune for the reception booking and—'

'Actually,' Hayley interrupted him again with a hard set to her mouth, '*I've* paid for everything so far, including the honeymoon.'

'Which won't go to waste,' Jasper said as he slung an arm around Hayley's waist. He looked down at her with a sexy smile, his dark eyes gleaming. 'I can't wait to spirit her away and spend every day and night of our honeymoon showing her how much I worship her.'

Hayley felt hot colour storm not only her cheeks but deep inside her body as well. It seeped like a scorching flow of lava into every secret place, making her feel as if her legs were going to melt into a liquid pool on the floor.

'Mr Caulfield—' the waiter smiled '—your table is ready. And the French champagne you ordered is on its way.'

'Thank you, Giovanni,' he said and turning back to Myles, he said, 'No hard feelings, mate.' His gaze flicked to the big-breasted blonde sitting opposite, giving her a wink before returning to Myles's goggled-eyed expression. 'But it looks like you're being more than adequately compensated for your broken engagement. *Ciao.*'

Hayley stumbled after him as he led her to their table, her ego feeling as if it had been stomped on by a pair of very large steel-capped working boots.

She sat down in the chair Jasper held out for her, her expression stormy as he took the chair opposite.

'That went pretty well, I thought,' he said with a twinkling smile.

She sent him a venomous glare without responding. How could he be so…so *amused* by this? She had just been let down in the most appalling way and he was laughing about it.

He leaned closer and said in a low, deep tone, 'Listen, baby girl, they're watching us like hawks. Relax and act like a woman who's been swept off her feet.'

Two big tears popped out of her eyes. 'I can't believe he's having an affair with *her.*' She sniffed and rummaged for a tissue, but gave up when Jasper discreetly handed her his handkerchief across the table. She blew her nose rather noisily and handed it back to him.

Jasper looked at it and grimaced. 'No, you keep it.'

Hayley poked it up her sleeve and sniffed again. 'She's not even attractive. And those breasts cannot possibly be real. And she wears so much makeup she looks like a…a street worker for God's sake!'

'Some men are such pushovers when it comes to temptation,' he said, shaking his head in mock dismay. 'She's not the first one he's played around with either.'

She flicked her napkin across her lap viciously and continued her infuriated tirade. 'Now I know why he was always putting off sleeping with me. He said it was because he wanted our first time to be on our wedding night. God, how could I have fallen for that? I must be stupid or something. No man wants to wait more than a date or two, let alone three months!'

Jasper frowned. 'What? You've only been going out with him three months?'

'Yes.' She looked across at him, blinking back tears. 'What's wrong with that?'

He sat back in his chair and gave her an ironic look. 'How can you possibly know if you want to spend the rest of your life with someone in three months?'

'I knew in three days that I wanted to marry him. He wanted the same things I wanted. A white wedding, babies and a lifelong commitment to making our marriage work.'

'That's bloody ridiculous! It's asking for trouble tying yourself to someone you don't know properly. He might have God knows what dark secrets in his background.'

She returned his look of irony, but added a curl of her lip. 'Like you, you mean?'

His dark brows snapped together. 'Shut up, Hayley. You don't know what you're talking about.'

'I see Miriam's new mother-in-law occasionally, you know,' she said with a defiant look. 'June Beckforth comes into the salon. She tells me all about *your* son. The one you wanted Miriam to abort.'

His jaw tightened. 'I did *not* ask her to do that.'

She rolled her eyes and affected a bored yawn, covering her mouth with her hand. 'Oh, dear…I am *so* tired of that old story,' she said.

'You don't know what you're talking about,' he ground out in a harsh undertone. 'I've got a good mind to—'

The waited approached with a bottle in his hand. 'Champagne for you, miss?'

'Yes…thank you…'

'Mr Caulfield.' The waiter turned to Jasper's glass and poured the fizzing bubbles into it. 'What are we celebrating this evening?'

Hayley flashed Jasper a fiery glance before smiling sweetly at the waiter. 'We're getting married,' she said with a husky purr. 'I've finally tamed the one man who said he was never going to get married. I think that's worth celebrating, don't you?'

'Indeed it is.' The waiter beamed. 'When's the wedding taking place?'

'In three weeks' time,' she said, still smiling dreamily, hoping to throw Jasper off balance. 'I'm so happy I can hardly stand it.'

'Congratulations to both of you,' the waiter said.

Jasper had to wait until the waiter had moved on before he could speak. 'Listen, little lady,' he growled. 'You can stop that lash fluttering routine right now. I want people to think this is a genuine match, not some trumped-up plan for you to make a fool out of me every chance you get.'

'No one's going to buy it, you know,' she said, glaring at him again.

'Your ex just did.'

'Only because I wanted him to,' she said with a lift of her chin. 'It was a matter of pride.'

'Yeah, well, I have my pride too, and if you so much as hint that our marriage is not real in every sense of the word I'll rip that salon out from under your feet faster than a waxing strip on a client's you know what.'

'You wouldn't dare!'

His eyes glinted warningly. 'Just watch me, cupcake.'

Another waiter came over with menus and two crusty bread rolls and set them on the table before moving off again.

Hayley took a hefty slug of her champagne before asking with eyes narrowed in suspicion, 'What do you mean "real in every sense of the word"? You're not expecting me to sleep with you, are you?'

He sent her a look of disdain. 'Absolutely not.'

Hayley hoped her surprise at the vehemence in his tone didn't show on her face. 'Good, because I wouldn't do it if you paid me.'

'I wouldn't do it if I *had* to pay you,' he countered. 'Firstly because I've never had to buy my way into a woman's bed before, and secondly it'd be a complete waste of money as I'm not the least bit attracted to a bad-tempered, spoilt little brat who should have grown up years ago.'

Hayley lowered her gaze, wondering why his emphatic statement had stung so much. Personality-clash issues aside, and even though she wasn't a vain sort of person, she knew she was OK-looking; clients told her so all the time, raving about her creamy complexion and thick dark curly hair and her blue-green eyes that changed colour with every mood. She knew her figure needed a little work, but her twice-weekly Pilates class was hopefully going to take care of that…well, it would once she got around to attending more regularly.

'Good, because I'm not attracted to you either,' she said, picking up her champagne again, hoping he couldn't see the lie for what it was. She might hate him but her body seemed to have a completely different angle on things. She could even feel it now, pulsing with awareness with him sitting so close.

'Better keep it that way,' he said. 'I wouldn't want you to get any ideas about making this marriage permanent. We only have to live together for a month. Any longer than that and we'd probably kill each other.'

She rolled her eyes in scorn. 'You really have had that ego of yours massaged a little too often, haven't you?'

'No more than any other Sydney billionaire bachelor.'

'Yeah, that'd be right.' She curled her lip again. 'It's your money they're after, you know.'

'And here I was thinking it was the mind-blowing sex,' he drawled.

Hayley knew her cheeks were bright red but carried on regardless. 'You know, I really hate men like you. You think that just because you've got money you can have whatever you want.'

'I *can* have whatever I want.'

'I can refuse to marry you, and then you won't,' she challenged him recklessly.

'You wouldn't dare.'

She sent him a glittering look. 'Oh, I dare all right,' she said.

Jasper leaned forward and captured one of her hands in his. 'Yes, you could, but there would be consequences. Do you need me to spell them out to you again?'

Hayley felt her stomach turn over itself as his long tanned fingers curled around hers, their latent strength unmistakable even though his hold was deceptively gentle.

His eyes were dark pools of mystery, shadows lurking there that secretly terrified her. He was a ruthless businessman. He had made his fortune as a property developer before he was out of his twenties and now, at thirty-three, was at his prime both professionally and personally.

He was handsome in a reckless bad-boy sort of way, his glossy black hair a shade or two darker than her own, not short, not long, not styled, not messy, but somewhere in between. It gave him a just-woke-up-just-had-bed-wrecking-sex sort of look, which somehow threatened Hayley's already shaky equilibrium. She felt on edge around him; she always had.

And now more so than ever.

'I've worked hard to build up my salon's reputation,' she said, tugging out of his hold. 'Gerald was so proud of what I'd achieved.'

'Only because he funded it.'

'He did not!' she said. 'He offered to but I wouldn't take it from him.' *Especially after what my mother did to him,* she tacked on mentally.

Jasper gave a grunt as he examined the menu. 'You were always good at winding him and Raymond around your little finger. No one else got a look-in once you came on the scene.'

'And that annoyed you, didn't it?' she asked. 'But it was your own fault. You seemed intent on annoying your father every chance you could.'

He tossed the menu to one side. 'You sucked up to him every chance you could, telling tales about me all the time, sticking your little snub nose into everyone else's business.'

Her jaw dropped. 'Snub nose?'

'Yeah, snub nose.'

She put a hand up to her nose and traced its contours. 'You really think it's that bad?' she asked.

Jasper frowned at the crestfallen look on her face. He was being a bastard, but somehow he couldn't help it when he was around her. She got under his skin. Made him feel things he didn't want to feel. One minute he wanted to throttle her for her stupid little tattle tales that had made his life hell, the next he wanted to kiss her senseless.

'Well, maybe not a snub exactly, but it does sort of tip up at the end a bit,' he said.

'And you think that's unattractive?' Her tone was suddenly full of insecurity. 'God, no wonder Myles wouldn't—'

'For God's sake, Hayley, your nose has nothing to do with it,' he said. 'He's a two-timing idiot and you're well rid of him. He slunk out of here twenty minutes ago, by the way, and didn't once look back this way. It has nothing to do with how you look. You look fine. Great, in fact. You've got great legs.'

Her expression brightened. 'You think so?'

He gave her a skewed smile. 'Yeah, shame about the nose, but the legs more than make up for it.'

She reached over and slapped his arm. 'You're a jerk,' she said.

'I know, but you love me anyway.'

'I do *not* love you,' she said with a flick of her dark mane of hair.

'I know, but only you and I know that,' he said. 'The rest of the world has to believe otherwise.'

'Does this mean you're going to have to tone down your monumental sexual activity over the next month?' she asked.

'How do you know about my sex life?'

She gave him a contemptuous look. 'I read the gossip pages occasionally. You're in every one, a different woman hanging off your arm every week. It's disgusting.'

'It's exciting, that's what it is,' he said with a twinkling smile. 'You're just jealous because Myles wasn't giving you any.'

She tightened her mouth at his crudity. 'How will you cope being celibate for a month?'

'Don't worry. I'll be discreet.'

She frowned at him, her heart suddenly squeezing painfully inside her chest. 'You mean you'll sleep with other women while living with me?'

He gave a casual lift of one shoulder. 'Why not?'

She sat back in her seat and folded her arms crossly. 'No way,' she said. 'If I'm going to agree to this ridiculous marriage I want you to play by *my* rules.'

'*I'm* the one making the rules, sweetheart,' he reminded her. 'But if you want to offer your services now and again I'd be more than happy to oblige.'

She gave him a scathing look. 'I thought you weren't the least bit attracted to me?'

He grinned at her cheekily. 'If the lights were off I think I could probably manage to perform.'

Hayley buried her head in her menu. The very last thing she wanted to think about was his sexual performance. Just sitting with his long legs so close to hers was enough to send her pulses soaring. She could just imagine how his hard, athletic body would feel pumping its desire into hers, his long limbs entrapping hers, his sensual mouth enticing hers into paradise.

She suppressed a tiny shiver and chose the most calorific item on the menu. She could always lose the weight, but the one thing she didn't want to lose was her heart.

And certainly not to him…

CHAPTER THREE

'SO WHERE DID you and Myles plan to go on honeymoon?' Jasper asked once their main meals had been cleared away.

'We were going to go to Green Island,' she said with a despondent slump of her shoulders.

'I meant what I said, you know,' he said. 'No point in wasting a perfectly good holiday.'

She looked up at him, her heart fluttering in sudden panic. 'You mean go together? Both of us? Alone?'

'Isn't that what newly married couples do?' he asked.

'I don't want to go with *you*,' she said, pouting. 'And certainly not on what was supposed to be *my* honeymoon.'

'You know something, Hayley,' he said with a thoughtful look, 'I don't think you were even in love with Myles.'

'Of course I was in love with him!'

He raised one dark brow at her. 'Was?'

'I mean I *am* still in love with him,' she amended quickly. 'I'm still processing the shock of finding out about his… affair…'

'He was totally wrong for you, you know,' he said. 'For a start he's old enough to be your father and, secondly, if he really loved you he wouldn't have taken your rejection without some sort of fight. He's clearly not strong enough for someone like you.'

She sent him a caustic glance over the top of her wineglass. 'Oh, and I suppose you know exactly who would be my perfect match, do you? You're hardly what I'd call a relationships expert,' she said. 'Anyway, what would you know what constitutes a good relationship? You've left a trail of broken hearts in your wake ever since you were a teenager.'

'So can I help it if I'm super-attractive to women?' he asked with a teasing smile.

She rolled her eyes into the back of her head and, reaching for her glass, drained it, adding as she placed it back on the table, 'You're not attractive to me.'

'I was once—don't you remember?'

Hayley wished she could permanently erase that one stupid incident from her mind and his for all time. He never missed a chance to remind her of her sixteenth birthday party when, under the influence of a little too much alcohol, she had thrown herself at him, begging him to make love to her. It had been the most embarrassing episode of her entire life. His cold disdain as he had unpicked her clinging fingers from him and escorted her out of his bedroom had tortured her ever since.

'Not even a little bit?' he taunted her.

'I prefer my men with a conscience,' she said with an imperious toss of her head. 'What you did to Miriam Moorebank was unforgivable.'

A flash of anger lit his dark brown gaze, his jaw becoming so tight she could see white tips appearing at the corners of his mouth.

'You know, I think I'm going to really enjoy being married to you,' he bit out. 'I'll finally get the chance to tame you as you should have been tamed a long time ago.'

A flicker of something hot and urgent pulsed between Hayley's thighs as his eyes clashed with hers. Her heart began to pick up its pace, the blood thrumming through her veins at

breakneck speed. Danger seemed to simmer in the air that separated them. She could feel it lurking there, like a leopard
hiding in the shadows, poised to pounce at its unsuspecting
prey.

'I haven't actually said I'll marry you,' she said as a last
show of defiance.

'I'm not going to give you a choice,' he said. 'I've been
doing a little research into your business affairs. You're currently stretched to the limit. And while your client turnover is
good and consistently growing, a sudden increase in rent just
now will tip you over the edge.'

Hayley felt her skin begin to prickle in agitation. She knew
he would do it and suffer no tweak of conscience about it.
Jasper Caulfield was not only ruthless in his personal relationships, but in business even more so. That was how he had
achieved the monumental success he had so far, all without a
single financial leg-up from his father, who had refused to offer
his support because of the shame Jasper had brought upon the
Caulfield name when he was eighteen.

'You'll have to drag me kicking and screaming to the altar,'
she warned him.

'I've already factored in that possibility.'

Hayley stared at him for a moment as her brain did a few
quick calculations. 'You set Myles up, didn't you?' she accused
him heatedly. 'You paid that woman to lure him away from
me.'

He leaned back in his chair and gave the red wine in his
glass a twirl. 'He didn't take too much luring,' he said
smoothly. 'One look at her cleavage and he was panting like a
terrier after a meaty bone.'

Hayley had trouble controlling her rage. It bubbled and
boiled inside her, every part of her twitching with the desire to
slap that supercilious smirk off his face.

Her hand reached for her glass but, as if he sensed where her mind was leading, he reached for the wine bottle and strategically moved it out of her reach.

'You bastard!' she said, her eyes flashing with twin flares of livid blue flame. 'I bet you paid that woman to break up my engagement! How could you do such a thing? *How could you?*'

'Contrary to the conclusion you've as usual so hastily jumped to, I did not have anything to do with Myles's affair. The real estate and property world is rather small. I happened to hear he was a bit of a womaniser when I was speaking with a mutual acquaintance. I thought I should warn you before you got your fingers burnt.'

'I don't believe you,' she shot back. 'That's exactly the sort of thing you'd do to get your own way.'

'Listen, sugar,' he drawled, 'it seems to me that if your ex-fiancé *could* be lured away from you by someone like Serena Wiltshire, then he definitely isn't the man for you, as I indicated earlier. If he was in love with you, no one, and I mean no one, no matter how attractive or determined, would be able to lead him away from you.'

Hayley knew deep down inside that what he said was reasonable but she didn't want him to be right.

She *hated* that he was right.

She *hated* him full stop.

'When you think about it I did you a favour,' he added. 'You found out what a weak person Myles was just in time. Imagine how painful it would have been to find out after you were married with a couple of kids.'

Jasper watched as she sank her teeth into her lower lip, her blue-green eyes misting over again, her small hands absently fidgeting with her glass. Something hard inside him shifted and softened but he couldn't for the life of him decide what it was.

She looked up at him again, her eyes liquid pools of shimmering blue and green. 'So you really didn't pay her to break up my engagement?'

He reached across the table and took one of her hands in his, curling his fingers around her smaller ones. 'No,' he said with a grim set to his features. 'She's not the first and I expect will not be the last. Some men develop a taste for that sort of thing.'

Hayley looked down at their joined hands, his long tanned fingers with their dusting of masculine hair in stark contrast to the creamy softness of hers.

Light and dark.

Hard and soft.

Man and woman.

Man and wife...

She pulled her hand away and wriggled in her seat in agitation as she forced her mind away from such traitorous thoughts. What was the matter with her? Surely one glass of wine couldn't suppress inhibition to that degree?

'I've asked Raymond to marry us,' Jasper inserted into the silence. 'But he didn't sound too keen on the idea given the circumstances.'

She pursed her mouth at him. 'I suppose you're going to ridicule Raymond for standing up for what he believes in. But at least he's a decent man who does his best for the community. So many men these days have turned their back on the priesthood, but he's made that huge sacrifice, and the very least you could do is respect him for it. Anyway, if he did take any money off you—unlike you—he wouldn't spend it on selfishly on himself, he would only use it for a good cause. He does an amazing job with the homeless youth in the inner city.'

Jasper's mouth tilted cynically. 'That's right,' he said. 'Everyone loves Raymond.'

'He visited Gerald almost daily in the weeks before he died, and yet you didn't bother to go out there once.'

'I didn't see the point,' he said. 'My father always preferred my brother, not to mention you. I only seemed to upset him every time I called, so I gave up in the end.'

'Why did you go out of your way to annoy him so much?' she asked. 'You seemed to relish in shocking him at every opportunity.'

A curtain seemed to come over his face as he reached to top up both of their glasses. 'My father liked to think he could control me,' he said. 'But I wasn't prepared to play the game.'

'You're playing now, though, aren't you?' she said. 'You're following the dictates of his will to the letter.'

His eyes met hers across the table. 'I want that property, Hayley,' he said. 'And nothing and no one is going to stand in my way to get it.'

'Except me,' she reminded him coolly.

His eyes glittered as they held hers. 'If you want to play dirty, darling, I'm all for it. I love nothing better than a damned good fight. But I should warn you that you are the one who has the most to lose. The financial security you've worked so hard for will be in jeopardy.'

It was on the tip of her tongue to say he wouldn't dare, but she stopped just in time.

He *would* dare.

'The very last thing I want to do is marry you,' she said staring into the blood-red contents of her glass.

'If it's any consolation to you I feel exactly the same way,' he said. 'But we only have to live together for a month. And it's the only way we will both get what we want.'

She raised her eyes to his once more. 'It seems to me you stand to gain much more from this enterprise than I do. You get to inherit Crickglades while I get a sum of money at the end.'

He studied her tense features for a moment. 'Were you surprised he didn't leave you more?'

'No, of course not…' She looked genuinely puzzled by his query. 'Why should I? I'm not a blood relative. I was just his stepdaughter and not for all that long at that.'

'All the same, it had been generally assumed he had left you the lot.'

'It was generally assumed by *you,* no one else,' she put in caustically. 'I never once asked Gerald for a thing. To tell you the truth I was surprised he didn't leave everything equally between you and Raymond.' A little frown interrupted the smoothness of her brow. 'He must have changed his mind at the last minute for some reason.'

'Perhaps he assumed Raymond would be well provided for by the church,' he said, and, after an almost undetectable pause, added, 'It's all my brother has ever wanted to do. For as long as I can remember he had his heart set on the priesthood.'

Something in his tone brought Hayley's gaze back to his. 'You admire him for it, don't you?' she said, unable to remove the element of surprise from her voice. 'I thought you didn't get on all that well.'

He met her look with equanimity. 'He's my older brother,' he said. 'We may have had our differences growing up, but what brothers don't? But, yes, I do admire him for sacrificing himself for others. It's not something everyone can or is prepared to do.'

Hayley ran a fingertip around the rim of her glass as she let the silence swirl about them momentarily. 'About the pre-nup thing…'

Jasper stiffened. 'What about it?'

'Your father insisted there wasn't to be one between us.'

'So?'

She met his gaze once more. 'As far as I see it you are in a very precarious situation,' she said, choosing her words with care. 'If I agree to this marriage between us, at the end of it I can legitimately strip you of, if not half, then a considerable portion of your assets.'

He clenched his jaw, making his cheekbones instantly sharpen, his mouth turning into a thin white line. 'I was right about you all along, wasn't I?' he said. 'My father was a blind fool. He thought you were nothing like your sleep-around money-hungry mother, but you're already counting the pennies, aren't you?'

Hayley wanted to defend herself but stopped just in time. Let him think she was after all she could get. What did it matter? He hated her anyway. Nothing she said was going to change that. But if any money did come her way she would give it to Daniel Moorebank, the son he had abandoned.

'I have decided I will marry you,' she said with a lift of her chin.

Jasper's dark eyes bored into hers. 'Why do I get the feeling I'm going to regret this?' he asked.

'As you say, we'll only have to live together for a month,' she reminded him. 'And it's not as if we have to spend every second of it together. You can live your life and I'll live mine. It will be over before we know it.'

He drummed his fingers on the table for a moment, his eyes still locked on hers. 'So you really are prepared to be my wife?'

'Yes, but we only have to share a house, not a bed.'

'True.'

'So whose house are we going to live in?' she asked.

'Mine, of course.'

Hayley felt her stomach drop. The thought of sharing his house made it all so terribly intimate. 'Why should I be the one to move?' she asked.

'You live in a little flat while I live in a harbourside mansion,' he said. 'End of discussion.'

She gritted her teeth, gearing herself up for another tussle, when she recalled a photograph she'd seen in the press of Jasper's Point Piper residence. Three of his neighbours were movie stars, and if that weren't enough inducement the lap pool, tennis court and in-house gym and sauna and spa were enough to make anyone think twice about rejecting a month living there rent free. Besides, as he'd said, it was a whole lot more spacious than her flat, which would perhaps make it easier for her to avoid him.

'OK,' she said. 'You win. I'll move in with you but we need to lay down some ground rules from the outset.'

He slung an arm over the back of his chair and lifted his wineglass to his mouth again. 'Fine by me,' he said.

'Firstly, I'm not doing the whole wife thing. I don't cook, I don't clean, I don't iron and I don't shop, or at least only for myself.'

'I have a housekeeper who does all that so that shouldn't be a problem,' he said. 'However, she will think it's a bit strange if we don't sleep together, but hopefully we can think of some excuse to allay her suspicions.'

'Tell her you snore. Lots of married couples don't share the same bed because of that little problem.'

'Good suggestion,' he said with a little smile lifting one edge of his mouth. 'That could work.'

'Secondly,' she continued, 'I expect to be able to have some sort of social life if you're going to continue seeing other women during our marriage.'

Jasper placed his glass back down on the table. 'No. Absolutely not.'

She stared at him. '*No?* What do you mean no?'

'I can't have my wife having it off with other men,' he said. 'I'm a high-profile person. What do you think the press would make of it? I'd be a laughing stock.'

'So what? It won't stop you achieving your goal of inheriting Crickglades at the end of the month,' she said.

His brows came together over his eyes. 'That's completely beside the point. No man likes to think of his wife entertaining other men behind his back. It's a matter of male pride.'

'What about my pride?' she asked. 'If you're off gallivanting with other women how am I supposed to feel?'

'I told you I'd be discreet.'

'What about a compromise?' she suggested.

His eyes narrowed slightly. 'What sort of compromise?'

'How about we both remain celibate for the month?'

His jaw dropped. 'You're kidding, right?'

She folded her arms across her chest and shook her head. 'Nope.'

She watched as he raked a hand through his thick black hair before using it to rub his jaw, the rasping sound of his hand moving over his evening shadow making her tummy feel as if someone had tickled it with a very long, soft feather.

'That's impossible,' he said. 'It's not natural.'

'Raymond doesn't seem to have any problem with it,' she pointed out. 'He says celibacy is an act of worship.'

'Celibacy is an act of madness,' he said in response. 'You surely can't be serious?'

She held his look without answering, her blue-green eyes sparkling with determination.

'Damn it,' he said with a rueful grimace. 'You *are* serious.'

'Take it or leave it,' she said. 'If you can hold out for a month I won't ask for half your assets at the end of our marriage. How's that for a deal?'

'It's like a lot of deals I've seen,' he remarked wryly. 'They look good on paper but when it comes to putting them in action it's often an entirely different ball game.'

'If you want Crickglades, then surely this is a small sacrifice to pay?' she said. 'After all, you're asking me to give up a month of my life, so I don't see why you shouldn't give up a month of yours too.'

He studied her for a moment, his dark eyes probing hers. 'You're doing this deliberately, aren't you?' he asked.

She fought back a smile. 'Think of it as long-service leave,' she said, blushing slightly. 'God knows you've been hard at it for years if what's written in the press is to be believed.'

'Yeah well, I guess you could say this is one time you can believe what you read in the press,' he said with a smug smile.

She shifted her eyes from his. 'Not that I read everything that's written about you or anything.'

'Of course not.'

She tossed her long hair behind one shoulder. 'I have much better things to do with my time than keep track of your sex life.'

'Of course you do,' Jasper said, still smiling. God, she was so damned cute when she blushed like that. Why hadn't he noticed that before? And the way her teeth bit into the soft cushion of her bottom lip, making him want to press his mouth to hers to see if it really was as soft as it looked. He could feel his blood surging in his groin just thinking about sliding his tongue through those pouting lips to taste her sweetness…

'I live a full life,' she went on, still trying to avoid his dark gaze. 'A very full life.'

'With no sex.'

Her eyes flew to his, her face on fire. 'That's not true!'

One dark eyebrow lifted in a perfect arc. 'But not with Myles, right?'

She lowered her eyes. 'I'm not a virgin, if that's what you're thinking,' she said, chewing her bottom lip for a second or two.

'I was beginning to wonder,' he said. 'But then I reminded myself you're twenty-eight years old. You must have done the deed with someone or several someones even if it wasn't with Myles.'

'It's really none of your business.'

'I guess not.'

Hayley wished she had a long list of lovers to brandish in his face, but the truth was there had only been the one and the experience had not exactly been one she'd been keen to repeat. She had felt immensely sorry for Warren Porter, who had fumbled his way through the encounter with too little finesse and far too much haste when they were both nineteen. He had apologised profusely when it was over, his face showing his shame at not being able to pleasure her sufficiently. She had patted his arm reassuringly, and, feeling more like his mother than his girlfriend, had told him she wasn't really ready for a serious relationship and that it wasn't his fault at all.

Somehow Hayley couldn't imagine Jasper Caulfield leaving any one of his lovers high and dry. He positively oozed sexual potency through every pore of his olive skin. His dark come-to-bed eyes were an incredible temptation, not to mention his sensual mouth that would surely make mincemeat of any woman's resolve to resist him. Just sitting opposite him sharing a meal had pushed her way out of her comfort zone. She could feel her skin reacting to his proximity, all the fine hairs on the back of her neck lifting every time those were-they-black-were-they-brown eyes connected with hers.

Her gaze dipped to his mouth and she swallowed as she saw his tongue snake out to taste the last of his wine off his lips. She could almost sense what his mouth would feel like on hers: it wouldn't be fumbling and awkward like Warren's, neither would it be the quick peck of greeting and farewell Myles had drifted into the habit of giving her lately. Jasper's mouth would be sensually commanding, his tongue determined as it mated intimately with hers.

'Would you like another glass of wine?' he asked into the stretching silence.

'Um…no…I think I've had more than enough,' she said pushing her glass away.

'You do look a little flushed,' he observed. 'What about dessert? Do you still have a sweet tooth? I seem to remember you had a bit of a thing for chocolate in the past.'

She grimaced in memory of her teenage binges. 'Only when I'm feeling a bit depressed.'

'So what about now?'

'What about now?' she asked.

He gave her a quizzical look. 'You're not feeling depressed?'

'No. Why should I?'

He looked at her for three or four pulsing seconds, his expression contemplative. 'Mmm…seems I was right,' he said musingly. 'You couldn't possibly have been in love with Myles. Isn't he worth a big chunk of Mississippi Mud Cake at the very least?'

Hayley sucked in her tummy and reached for the dessert menu perched between them. 'You're right,' she said with a defiant toss of her head. 'To hell with the calories; it's not as if I have to look fabulous on my wedding day now.'

He laughed, the deep, rich rumble doing far more damage to Hayley's tummy than any amount of Mud Dake could ever do.

'That's my girl,' he said, winking at her. 'You always were a pushover when it came to temptation.'

She bent her head to the menu again, doing her level best to ignore the racing of her heart at the thought of being tempted by him on a daily basis for a month.

Four weeks living with him—alone.

How on earth was she going to stand it?

CHAPTER FOUR

'YOUR FIANCÉ IS here to see you,' Lucy informed Hayley a week later.

Hayley looked up from the paperwork she'd been trying to sort out for the last hour. 'Myles?'

Lucy's brows lifted slightly. 'Er…actually, no…' she said. 'The new one: the gorgeous totally sexy and irresistible Jasper Caulfield one.'

Hayley felt her colour begin to rise and lowered her gaze back to the accounts and shuffled them absently. 'Oh, *that* one…'

Lucy perched on the edge of Hayley's desk. 'Are you really going to go through with it?' she asked. 'I mean, a marriage of convenience is still a marriage, right?'

'Only on paper.'

Lucy looked doubtful. 'You reckon you and he won't be tempted somewhere along the way to make it a real one?'

'Absolutely not,' Hayley insisted, wondering if she had answered a little too quickly and adamantly to be convincing. The truth was she hadn't slept properly for days thinking of what she had agreed to in entering a temporary marriage with Jasper. But as far as she saw it there really wasn't much choice in the matter. She'd run her own checks and found out he did in fact now own the entire block of real estate where her salon was situated, which meant his threats of a hefty rent increase were now disturbingly real.

'Have you told anyone apart from me that it's not going to be a proper marriage?' Lucy asked.

'No, and I'd appreciate it if you kept it a secret for as long as possible. I don't want Myles to find out. I want to grind his pride in the dust like he did to me. God, when I think of that woman—grrrrrr!'

'You know, I never did think he was right for you,' Lucy said examining her French manicured gel nails for a moment.

'What makes you say that?'

Lucy's expression was serious when she returned her gaze to Hayley's. 'I know you probably don't want to admit it, but ever since I met you when we started at the beauty academy together you've been craving security. I guess it comes from never having a father and your mum being so…' she blushed faintly and went on '…well, you know what I mean. You've told me enough about her for me to know how hard it was for you growing up with her flitting between unsavoury men all the time. Myles was more like a father-figure to you than a life partner.'

Hayley gave her bottom lip a little nibble before releasing a tiny, barely audible sigh. She wasn't sure she needed her best friend to agree so harmoniously with her worst enemy. 'I'd better go and see what Jasper wants,' she said rising to her feet.

'You know, I'm really starting to like him,' Lucy said. 'Apart from his great looks he seems to have a brain instead of an ego between his ears.'

Hayley gave her a wry glance. 'He's certainly got an ego, but I can assure you it's definitely not between his ears.'

Jasper looked up from the magazine he was reading when Hayley came out to Reception. He tossed it to one side and got to his feet, his sudden increase in height making her feel minuscule in spite of her three-inch heels.

'Hi, sweetheart,' he said. 'Fancy a quick coffee with your favourite fiancé?'

'I've got clients booked all afternoon,' she said, surreptitiously placing her right hand over the appointment book where her afternoon had been blanked out so she could see to the most pressing accounts.

He picked up her hand and, turning over her palm, pressed a kiss on the sensitive underside of her thumb, his dark eyes holding hers like a powerful magnet. Hayley felt her stomach drop like an out-of-control elevator, her legs turning to water as his tongue came out and tasted the centre of her palm.

'Mmm…what's that flavour?' he asked, sniffing her palm.

'Um…' She sucked in a prickly little breath. 'It's probably vanilla hand cream…'

He released her hand and looked down at the appointment book. 'Well, what do you know?' he said. 'You've got the whole afternoon free. Lucky me.'

'I'm supposed to be doing paperwork,' she said, tightening her mouth.

'It can wait. I have something to give you.'

'You can give it to me here,' she said.

'What I want to give you demands absolute privacy,' he insisted.

Her eyes widened a fraction. 'I hope you're not getting any funny ideas about our relationship,' she said, gripping the counter to steady herself from the onslaught of his smouldering dark gaze.

The door pinged open behind him and Hayley had to strip the glare off her face and smile past Jasper's broad shoulder as one of Lucy's regulars came in. 'Hello, Mrs French,' she said. 'I—I'll just let Lucy know you're here.'

Mrs French smiled up at Jasper as Hayley went out back. 'You must be Hayley's new fiancé. I've heard all about you. I must say you're a big improvement on the last. I thought he was far too old for her.'

Jasper smiled down at the older woman. 'I'm very glad you approve.'

'Oh, I do,' Mrs French said. 'That dear girl needs a man with a bit of get up and go in him. It always seemed to me Myles Lederman's get up and go got up and went a long time ago.'

Hayley came back out to hear Jasper chuckling with amusement and sent him a cold little look as Lucy ushered her client through to the treatment room.

'What's so funny?' she asked.

'Nothing,' he said, still smiling.

She pursed her mouth at him again. 'Let's get this over with,' she said, and retrieved her bag from beneath the front counter. 'But I can't be away long. Lucy's fully booked and our part-time receptionist is off today.'

'This won't take long,' he said, and led her out to his car parked outside.

Hayley strapped herself into the seat belt, trying not to notice how very close his muscular thigh was to hers with only the gear stick to separate them.

She felt herself being thrown back in the seat by the G-force of the car as it surged out of the parking space and she clutched at the arm-rest in alarm. 'Do we have to go so fast?' she gulped as he shifted his way through the gears.

He flicked a playful glance her way. 'You said you were short of time.'

'You don't have to break the speed limit.'

'I won't break any rules,' he said, and turned back to the traffic, 'or at least not unless I'm tempted way beyond my endurance.'

She turned in her seat to look at him. 'What on earth do you mean by that?'

He gave her one of his enigmatic smiles. 'Just don't tempt me, baby girl,' he warned. 'Otherwise you might find yourself flat on your back with me showing you just how good my get up and go is.'

Hayley felt the scorch of embarrassment firing in her cheeks. 'You wouldn't dare!'

'You know all about me and your little dares,' he said.

'We made an agreement,' she reminded him tersely.

'I know, but the way I see it living together is going to test that agreement to the limit.'

'I don't see how since you made it perfectly clear you're not the least bit attracted to me.'

His gaze swung back in her direction. 'You're not my usual type. *However*—'

'Why? Because I've got a brain?' she cut him off scornfully. 'Your last three girlfriends had shoe sizes bigger than their IQ's.'

'So you've been doing a little research on me, have you?' Jasper asked with a secret smile.

She gave him a disgusted look. 'You've been described in the press with three s words: shallow, self-serving and sexy.'

'Well, there you go,' he said. 'At least you know what you're getting in a husband.'

'You're not going to be my husband, not really.'

'That's another thing I've been thinking about,' he said. 'Have you told anyone our relationship is not the real deal?'

She shifted uncomfortably in her seat. 'I told Lucy because she's a close friend, but that's all.'

'Good. I think it's best if we maintain an illusion of normality. For one thing you don't want your ex-fiancé to suspect anything's amiss, and secondly I have a big property negotiation I'm working on in the Southern Highlands. The couple who own the land I've got my eye on are pretty old-school. They've been married for fifty-odd years and don't want to sell their land to just anyone. They've been cagey about the deal for weeks but as soon as they heard I was engaged their entire attitude changed towards me. They even want to meet you.'

Hayley looked at him in consternation. 'Do you think that's a good idea? I mean, I'm not sure I'll be able to be that convincing.'

'It'll be a pushover,' he reassured her. 'All you have to do is gaze up at me adoringly like you used to do when you were a teenager.'

Hayley found her memory drifting back to when the five years that separated them had seemed such a huge amount of time compared to now. She had still been sleeping with her collection of soft toys while he had been sleeping with any number of local girls, his reputation as a bad boy spreading far and wide. He had been in and out of trouble so many times she suspected he had done it deliberately to punish his father for having left his mother for hers.

When Kathryn Caulfield had been killed in a car accident a few weeks after Gerald had married her mother, Eva, Jasper had disappeared for months on end, cutting off all contact with his father.

Jasper brought the car to a halt and came around to open the door for her. 'Welcome to what will be your home for the next month,' he said.

Hayley unfolded herself from the car and looked around. His residence looked even more impressive than the gossip pages had indicated. The house was huge, built on three levels as far as she could make out, the garden beautifully landscaped to make the most of the spring sunshine, the sun dappling the surface of the lap pool like sparkling diamonds. A grass tennis court dominated one corner of the generous block and as they moved into the house itself the views over the harbour brought her breath to a standstill.

'It's…fabulous…' she breathed in wonder, turning around to look at the open-plan layout.

Plush leather sofas that seemed bigger than her entire flat were positioned to make the most of the view and a well-stocked bar was to one side of the massive entertainment system that lined one wall. The kitchen and dining area flowed into one, the space accommodating at least twenty if not more.

'It's all right I guess,' he said tossing his keys onto the nearest surface.

'All right?' She gaped at him. 'This is the most wonderful house I've ever seen!'

'Don't get too attached to it,' he said as he bent down to retrieve something off the marble-top coffee-table. 'It's only for a month, remember.'

'I haven't forgotten,' she responded tartly.

He came over with a small velvet box in his hands and handed it to her. 'I thought since we're pretending this is all above board you should have an engagement ring.'

Hayley stared down at the tiny box in her hands and slowly opened it, her breath catching when she saw the bright glitter of a cluster of diamonds nestling in amongst the royal-blue velvet.

She wasn't sure what to say. It was surely an unnecessary expense given their marriage was to be temporary, but, in spite of that, she felt incredibly touched that he had chosen such an exquisite ring for her.

'I'm not sure if it will fit.' His deep voice broke the silence. 'I had to guess the size.'

She slipped it over her knuckle with ease. 'It does,' she said, looking up at him with amazement. 'That was a good guess.'

His eyes locked with hers.

'It's beautiful…but you really shouldn't have bothered,' she said, feeling as if something inside her chest had rearranged itself. 'It's not as if this is a real marriage or anything. I'll have to give this back to you when it's over.'

'No.' His hand came over hers, holding the ring in place, so much so she could feel the sharp edges of the diamonds pinching her skin, his eyes dark and serious as they held hers. 'No. I want you to keep it. Think of it as a gift for how you're helping me.'

'I—I can't accept such an expensive gift from you,' she said, twisting out of his grasp. 'It wouldn't be right.'

He captured her hand again and closed her fingers over her palm. 'No, Hayley,' he said. 'I want you to have this.'

'Jasper…I…' She moistened her mouth with her tongue, her heart leaping about in her chest. 'I don't know what to say…'

'How about for a change you don't say anything?' he suggested, pulling her a little closer.

She felt the buckle of his belt against the softness of her tummy, his strong thighs like tree trunks against the shivering leaves of hers.

'W-what are you doing?' she asked, trying to pull back, but her efforts only succeeded in bringing her pelvis closer to his, her yielding softness against his unmistakable hardness.

'I'm thinking about kissing you,' he said, his dark gaze dipping to her mouth, brushing it like a feather. 'In fact I've been thinking about it for days.'

'W-why would you want to do that?' Her voice sounded more like a squeak than her usual even tones.

'I kind of figure we're going to have to do it occasionally,' he said, still looking down at her mouth, his thumbs slowly stroking the undersides of her wrists.

Hayley unconsciously ran her tongue over her dry lips. 'D-do what?'

'Kiss each other.'

'But…but why?'

'Because we'll be married to each other and people will expect it.'

She swallowed. 'I don't think we should take things to that extreme… I mean a quick peck on the cheek now and again will do…won't it?'

'No.'

Her stomach tilted. 'No?'

'If we are going to convince people this is a real marriage, then we're going to have to put in some sort of effort to get the body language between us right.'

'I don't think I—'

'You can go first if it makes you feel more comfortable,' he suggested.

'Me?'

'Yes. You kiss me and then I'll kiss you.'

Hayley's eyes flicked uncertainly to his mouth.

'Come on, Hayley,' he said, the whisper of his words caressing her lips as he pulled her even closer. 'Do it. I dare you.'

She stood up on tiptoe and pressed a brief brush-like kiss to the side of his mouth. 'There,' she said, her breathing a little shallow and uneven. 'I did it.'

'Now it's my turn.' His hands moved from her wrists to rest on her hips, the pressure of his hold just enough to tip her forwards as his mouth came down, as if in slow motion, until finally she felt the heated imprint of his lips along the softness of hers.

When she thought about it later, she realised there was nothing that could have prepared her for the feel of his tongue stroking the seam of her lips in its determined quest for entry. Heat exploded inside her as he thrust through when her mouth opened on her little startled gasp of response, the stroke and glide of him against her tongue sending her into a heart-stopping spiral of feeling. Her stomach began to crawl with desire, her skin prickling all over with it, her whole body alive with the need to feel more of his devastating touch. His tongue swooped and dived again for hers, calling it into a sensuous dance that mimicked the most intimate of embraces, her lower body responding with liquid warmth as he pressed her even closer to his hardness. She felt the ridge of his erection against her belly, its probing force a heady reminder of how incredibly experienced he was and how vulnerable she was to the temptation of his possession.

His hands moved from her hips upwards to settle just below her breasts, not quite touching but near enough for her to feel the aching tightness of expectation in her nipples pushing against the lace of her bra. She wanted to feel the warmth of his palms on her without the barrier of her clothes. She wanted to feel his hot, moist mouth sucking on her, his tongue rolling over each nipple in turn.

She whimpered softly as he deepened the kiss even further, his hard body pulsing against hers until her legs felt as if they were going to melt beneath her. Her arms moved to encircle his waist, her hands shaping the firmness of his taut buttocks in increasing boldness. She felt his leaping response against her, the sound of his deep groan rumbling in his throat signalling she was having much the same effect on him as he was on her.

He lifted his mouth from hers, his dark eyes glittering. 'Well, I guess that clears up that little matter, then,' he said with a little wry smile.

'What do you mean?' she asked, extracting herself from his hold with cold deliberation.

'You couldn't possibly have been in love with Myles Lederman. You wouldn't have responded to me like that if you were.'

She gave him a furious look. 'For your information I've

cried myself to sleep for the past week. I don't think I'll ever get over Myles's betrayal.'

'Well it's about time you did,' he said. 'He was only marrying you because he thought you were going to inherit the bulk of my father's estate.'

Hayley's mouth fell open. 'That's a despicable lie!'

He jerked one shoulder up and down as if he didn't care what accusation she levelled at him. 'I've recently run some checks on his background,' he said. 'He's up to the eyeballs in debt. It's my guess he knew you were very close to my terminally ill father, and, since it's been no secret in the press that I wasn't exactly on good terms with the old man, Lederman decided to move in for the kill. He swept you off your feet within weeks, fast-tracking your wedding so he could get his hands on your inheritance.'

She swung away in disgust. 'I don't believe a word of this. You're making it up.'

'I was speaking to Max, the part-time gardener out at Crickglades,' he went on. 'It seems Gerald didn't like your choice of fiancé although he didn't think it his place to say so to you. Duncan Brocklehurst confirmed that the will had been changed a few days before he died.'

Hayley turned back to look at him in bewilderment. 'So what you're saying is Gerald preferred me to marry *you* rather than Myles?'

'I guess he was thinking along the lines of better the devil you know than the one you don't,' he said. 'One assumes he thought I wouldn't go as far as to rip you off and break your heart in the process.'

She frowned as she tried to take it all in. 'But Gerald knew how much we hated each other... Why would he force a marriage between us?'

'It was probably his idea of a sick joke,' he said. 'He knew very well what my views on marriage are, having put pressure on me before. Even a month living as husband and wife is going to seem like a lifetime. But I didn't have to go along with his plans; I could have walked away without a cent. Raymond would have got the lot and you and I would have been left out in the cold.'

Her eyes came back to his. 'But you wanted Crickglades,' she said. 'And were prepared to do whatever it took to get it.'

'Yes,' he said, and reached for his keys, his jaw stiff with determination. 'That's exactly right. I want Crickglades.'

'Why do you want it so much?' she asked with a puzzled frown. 'I thought you hated the place. You left as soon as you got the chance, hardly even coming home to visit your father more than once or twice a year.'

'I *do* hate the place,' Jasper said with emphasis. 'It has too many memories I would rather forget.' Memories of Eva Addington prancing about his mother's beloved house and garden, changing the decorating to fit her lurid taste, flirting with anything in trousers, including himself on one occasion. The property he had loved as a child had been tainted and he couldn't wait to bring it back to what it had been when his mother had made it a home instead of a house.

'So what are you going to do with it when you get it?' she asked, her tone liberally laced with censure. 'Raze it to the ground and build hundreds of stupid town houses on it?'

'What do you think I'm going to do with it?' he asked with a curl of his lip. 'Keep it for sentimental reasons?'

Hayley followed him back out to the car, her brain struggling to make sense of his motivations. Jasper wanted Crickglades but he'd made it perfectly clear he didn't want her. She wasn't sure why that should hurt so much. She had battled with him for years so it should be no surprise he would resent being tied to her, albeit temporarily, but it did hurt.

It hurt a whole lot more than it should.

CHAPTER FIVE

JASPER SWUNG HIS gaze to the silent figure beside him on the way back to the salon. He felt a bit of a heel for having to be the one to burst her bubble over her ex-fiancé, but he reassured himself she would get over it in time, if she hadn't already.

He was still feeling a little intrigued over her reaction to the ring he'd bought her. He had assumed she would have grasped at it greedily, counting the diamonds and rushing off to have it valued at the first opportunity as her mother Eva had done, but instead her eyes had shone with tears and her bottom lip had trembled as if she had been deeply affected by his gesture.

He could still taste her in his mouth, her response to him surprising him considering how much she claimed to detest him. He wasn't so sure he was ready to examine too closely his response to her, however. He had spent years avoiding the temptation of her young womanly body, but, no matter what he did to counteract it, her ripe curves still heated his blood whenever he was within touching distance.

'If you're free this weekend I thought we could do a quick run down to this property I'm interested in,' he said into the silence. 'You can meet the Hendersons, the couple I was telling you about.'

'Right at this point in time I don't feel like going anywhere with you,' she said with a little pout.

'Listen, Hayley, don't go shooting the messenger. I only told you what you would have found out given more time. As I said the other day, I've saved you a lot of future heartbreak.'

She sent him a brittle glance. 'I bet you're sitting there gloating right now, aren't you? You probably think it's been one big joke to destroy my ego in one fell swoop.'

'I did no such thing. Besides, I would have thought I gave your ego a massive boost back there when I kissed you. I can't remember a time when I was so turned on so quickly. It must be that perfume you're wearing.'

Hayley refused to be mollified by his somewhat backhanded compliment. 'I hope you're not going to get into the habit of using me to satisfy your animal urges,' she said.

He gave a little snort. 'You've been listening to too many of my brother's sermons.'

'At least he has a moral code,' she tossed back.

'And I don't?'

'You're like a lot of other deadbeat dads out there,' she said. 'You sow your wild oats and leave the women to reap the harvest all alone. Miriam Moorebank has struggled all her life because of what you did to her. Her mother-in-law told me how hard things are for her now.'

He flicked an angry glance her way. 'If you want to walk the rest of the way back to the salon then carry on the way you're going.'

'I'd rather walk than suffer your presence,' she said.

The car swerved to the left and before she knew what was happening he had reached across her and opened her door, his arm brushing against her breasts.

'OK, then,' he said. 'Out you get.'

She sucked in an angry breath. 'It's at least an hour's walk from here.'

'The exercise will do you good.'

'I'm not wearing the right shoes.'

'Get out of the car, Hayley.'

'No, I will not get out of the car!' she shouted at him, suddenly so close to tears she felt them bubbling at the back of her throat. She brushed at her eyes but it was too late. She put her head in her hands and began to sob.

Jasper let out a stiff curse. 'Damn it. I wish you wouldn't do that,' he growled as he reached out a hand to the back of her neck and pulled her into his chest, his nostrils flaring to take in more of the spring-garden fragrance of her shampoo. 'I'm sorry. I didn't mean to make you cry.'

She lifted her head out of her hands to send him an accusatory glare. 'Yes, you did,' she said, hiccupping. 'You've done nothing but upset me from the moment you barged into the salon and insisted I marry you. You blackmailed me, holding my business over my head until I can't sleep at night, and then you went and…and *kissed* me! How the hell am I supposed to cope with all that?'

His mouth twisted ruefully. 'I didn't think it was *that* bad a kiss.'

'You only did it to prove how weak I am.'

'You're not weak,' he said. 'Just human that's all.'

'I don't even *like* you,' she said. 'I've never liked you.'

'You don't have to like me—you just have to marry me.'

'I don't know what Gerald was thinking of leaving things like this,' she said brushing at her eyes. 'It's not as if I was expecting anything out of his will, but this is crazy. I feel like a pawn in a stupid game.'

Jasper looked at her while she was occupied with mopping up her tears. Could his father have been right after all? What if Hayley was completely different from her mother? What if she was as sweet and innocent as Gerald had always believed her to be? If so she was in danger of being hurt even more than Myles had hurt her when their temporary marriage came to its inevitable end. He didn't intend staying married to her any longer than he had to.

That was the deal.

Four weeks of living with Hayley to get back what was stolen from his mother. And even though she was no longer alive, he owed it to her to restore the house and garden to its former glory; then, and only then, would he feel that the avaricious presence of that slut Eva Addington would be finally eradicated.

'If there was any other way of achieving my goal I would do it, Hayley,' he said heavily. 'But this is the only way.'

'This is going to be the longest month of my life,' she said with another pout.

Jasper settled back in his seat and put the car into gear as he responded dryly, 'You and me too, baby.'

Hayley had fully intended to refuse to accompany Jasper to the country property on the following Sunday, but every time she went to pick up the phone to cancel she caught sight of the engagement ring he'd bought her and changed her mind. It suited her hand perfectly, the diamonds catching the light with every movement of her fingers. She still didn't understand why he'd gone to the trouble of buying her such a beautiful ring when everything about their relationship was so ugly.

There had been a time when she had dreamed of being married to Jasper for real, but such foolishness had long been put aside. She knew he was wary of commitment, his playboy lifestyle suggested he wasn't interested in marriage and babies—even the one he'd fathered—while lately she had been thinking of little else. Her biological clock had been ticking quietly in the background until her last birthday, when the volume had gone up to a deafening roar, keeping her awake at night in writhing fits of panic that time was running out.

She wondered now if that was why she had rushed into her relationship with Myles, clutching at the lifeline with both hands, knowing deep down that if she didn't do something she would end up doing nothing. She'd thought she had loved him, she had certainly enjoyed his company and he had seemed to want the same things in life as she did. On their very first date he'd mentioned kids and kittens and puppies, which had worked like a charm; she never could walk past a pram or a pet shop without a quick adoring peek.

The sound of Jasper's powerful car pulling up outside reverberated through the thin walls of her flat and she twitched the curtain aside to sneak a look at him. He unfolded his tall frame from the car, his black hair shiny in the bright spring sunshine, his white casual shirt teamed with dark blue jeans emphasising his spectacular fitness. His skin was a deep olive tan, which never seemed to fade in spite of the cold winter Sydney had just experienced. No doubt he'd been sunning himself at a tropical resort with a host of bikini-clad women while his father had drawn his last breath, she thought with a deep twinge of resentment.

She turned from the window and, scooping up her bag and cardigan in case the light breeze grew cold later, opened the door just as he was climbing the stairs to her floor.

'Nice to know how eager you are to see me,' he said with a teasing light in his dark eyes.

She gave him a quelling look. 'Actually,' she said in a lowered tone, 'my neighbour is a nurse currently on night duty. Your car made enough noise without you ringing the doorbell as well.'

He led the way to the car and waited until they were on their way before he spoke again. 'I've spoken again to Raymond about the ceremony.'

'Oh?'

'Apparently he's got another wedding to do but I can't help feeling he's relieved he doesn't have to be a party to this set-up.'

'I guess he's right in a way when you think about it,' she said. 'We're not exactly doing this for the right reasons. Marriage is meant to be for life.'

'What a pity your mother didn't share your view,' Jasper said with a curl of his lip.

He felt her stiffen as if the mention of her mother upset her and, flicking a quick glance her way, felt his chest tighten again when he saw what those small white teeth were doing to her bottom lip.

'Sorry,' he said after a lengthy pause.

'It's fine,' she said, looking down at her hands. 'I understand how you feel about my mother. I really do.'

'Have you seen her lately?' he asked, frowning at the way she was twirling her engagement ring almost agitatedly.

'No…'

He waited for a three-or-four beat silence to pass before he said, 'I would prefer it if she didn't come to the wedding.'

'I understand…' she said. 'She wasn't invited to my wedding to Myles either.'

There was another little silence.

'He's a creep, Hayley,' he said. 'A first class honours creep who was using you.'

'So what does that make you then?'

He drew his lips together tightly. 'I'm not using you.'

'Yes you are. That little kiss routine the other day was part of it. You think you can sweet talk me into not taking half your assets when our marriage is over, but it won't work. I hate you and I don't see that anything you can do, including buying me an outrageously expensive ring to butter me up, is going to change that.'

He shifted the gears with unnecessary force and overtook a stream of cars with a roar of the engine. 'You think that's why I bought you that ring?'

'Isn't it?'

'No,' he said. 'The truth is I took one look at the ring Lederman had given you and thought what a rotten cheapskate he was. I might not be marrying you for the best reasons in the world, but I thought you at least deserved real diamonds.'

Hayley turned away so he couldn't see the colour flooding her cheeks. 'It *was* a real diamond,' she said, but she knew her voice lacked conviction.

He snorted again. 'Sure it was.'

She turned and looked out of the window rather than face his derision. 'I'd rather have a fake diamond from a man who loved me than a whole bunch of real ones from a man who doesn't,' she said.

'Myles loved the prospect of getting his hands on your money, not you,' Jasper said. 'At least I haven't lied to you about my feelings. I feel the same way about you I always have.' *Now isn't that the truth?* he thought to himself. Desire hot and strong was keeping him awake at night just as it had done ever since she'd sprouted a chest and a kissable pout all those years ago.

She curled her lip. 'Oh, *please,* spare me another bludgeoning blow to my ego.'

He let out a very rude swear word. 'I'd like to do more than bludgeon your ego, young lady,' he muttered.

'You put one hand on me and I'll make you pay for it,' she threatened.

He threw her a stinging look. 'I'm already paying for it, sweetheart.'

Hayley didn't bother asking him what he meant. She wasn't sure she really wanted to know. She sat back stiffly in her seat and waited in silence for the journey to be over.

CHAPTER SIX

THE COUNTRY PROPERTY Jasper turned into some time later was accessed by a long winding gravel driveway lined on both sides with tall poplar trees, their bright new spring growth shivering in the fresh breeze.

The homestead at the end of the driveway was a colonial sandstone building with a sprawling cottage garden that seemed to fill every available space, the sweet scent of alyssum and early blooming roses filling the air as soon as Hayley stepped out of the car.

'Wow!' She looked around with wonder. 'What a beautiful place. Why on earth do they want to sell it?'

She received her answer as soon as the front door of the homestead opened to reveal a grey-haired woman in her early seventies standing behind a wheelchair where a man a few years older was sitting, his right arm lying uselessly across his lap.

Jasper took her hand and, giving her fingers a quick squeeze, said in a low tone, 'Don't forget, you're madly in love with me, right?'

She gave him a tight smile. 'Right.'

Mrs Henderson stepped from the verandah and took Hayley's hand. 'You must be the lovely fiancée Jasper has been telling us all about. My name is Pearl and this is my husband, Jim.'

'I'm very pleased to meet you both,' Hayley said, and reached to shake Jim's left hand to spare him the embarrassment of trying to lift his damaged one.

Jim Henderson mumbled something inaudible, his stroke-ravaged body tearing at Hayley's heartstrings. She leaned down to his level and asked him to repeat it, this time managing to make out what he'd said.

Pearl Henderson gave an approving smile and ushered them all indoors. 'I've made scones,' she announced. 'I thought we could have a cup of tea before Jasper shows you around the property.'

'That would be lovely,' Hayley said, breathing in the fresh fragrance of furniture polish as they went indoors.

The house was beautifully maintained, the furniture looking as if it had watched over several generations of Hendersons. Even the rugs on the timber floors bore the imprint of thousands of footsteps over the passage of time.

'This is such a beautiful home,' she said as Pearl Henderson handed her a cup and saucer. 'You must be feeling very sad to be leaving it.'

A shadow passed over Pearl's face as she pushed the milk and sugar closer so Jasper and her husband could reach it. 'It's time to move on,' she said. 'Jim's stroke has made things difficult to manage the outside work. We lost our only son a few years ago…otherwise he would have carried on the tradition. There have been Hendersons on this property for six generations.'

'I'm so sorry…' Hayley said, feeling the couple's pain like a silent presence in the room.

Pearl forced a smile to her lips as she passed the scones around. 'Of course, we're delighted now that Jasper is going to buy it,' she said. 'We weren't going to sell it to just anyone. I don't want our home bulldozed down to make way for shoebox town houses.'

Hayley did her best to keep her eyes from straying in Jasper's direction. What had he told the Hendersons? she wondered. He surely hadn't lied to them in order to secure the property? What would he want with several thousand acres of land unless to redevelop it to make the sort of money he normally made on such transactions? That was after all why he wanted his father's property Crickglades, which wasn't even a quarter of the size of this one.

'When he told us he was looking for somewhere to spend his weekends once he got married we reconsidered,' Pearl continued. 'This place is crying out for a young family to make it come alive again.'

Hayley very nearly choked on a crumb of scone and quickly gulped at her tea to disguise it.

'It's very good of you both to give me first offer,' Jasper said. 'I fell in love with this place the first time I saw it.'

Jim gave him a lopsided smile and mumbled something Hayley understood to be approval.

'Will you run cattle or sheep, do you think?' Pearl asked as she passed the home-made raspberry jam to him. 'We sold all our livestock a few months back, but with the spring growth it seems a shame to have it go to waste.'

'I'll appoint a manager to sort it out,' Jasper said, generously spreading a scone with the thick jam. 'I don't know much about farming, but I'm willing to learn.'

Hayley couldn't wait for morning tea to be over so she could go outside and challenge him. *Willing to learn indeed!*

Pearl began to clear the tea things a short time later. 'Why don't you take Hayley outside and show her the river walk?' she suggested. 'It's lovely at this time of year with the willows sprouting their new growth. When you get back we can finalise the details of the sale. Jim and I have the paperwork ready. We met with the lawyer the other day.'

'I'd love to see the river walk,' Hayley said, springing out of her chair and grabbing at Jasper's hand.

She waited until they were out of earshot and view of the house before she lambasted him. 'How could you lie to those poor old people?' She put her hands on her hips and mimicked him. '*I'm willing to learn about farming.* You unfeeling selfish bastard. How could you?'

'I'm not lying,' he said evenly. 'I am interested in learning a bit about farming.'

'Since when?' she asked.

'I thought it might be interesting to diversify my financial interests.'

'You're a property developer. You wouldn't know a cow or a sheep if you bumped into one,' she said. 'I know what you're up to and I won't be a part of it. You're going to buy this place under false pretences and then chop it up and develop it.'

'You're entitled to your opinion, but I can assure you that's not what I intend to do,' he said, walking towards the sinuous curve of the river in the distance.

Hayley had to trot to keep up. 'I hope you're not lying to me, Jasper,' she puffed. 'I would hate to think I was helping to deceive the Hendersons.'

He stopped to look down at her, an ironic smile tilting his mouth sideways. 'But you are helping to deceive them, baby girl,' he said. 'You're pretending to be in love with me and doing a damn fine job of it too.'

Hayley started to move away, but he snagged her arm and pulled her back to face him. She met his eyes, her stomach giving a little kick of excitement as his hands slid down her arms, his long, strong fingers encircling her wrists.

She suddenly felt exposed and vulnerable under his dark, intense scrutiny. She wondered if he had somehow guessed her real feelings, the feelings she was trying to hide from herself, let alone him. She had been fighting it for days, the attraction she'd thought had died twelve years ago with his cold dismissal, but instead it had leapt back into vibrant life, threatening to take over her common sense all over again.

He was standing so close she could smell his skin and the lemony notes of his aftershave that clung to it lightly. She could feel the pull of his pelvis as if he had a magnet attached to his belt that was luring her into intimate contact with him. She felt herself tilting towards him, her legs swaying as if they had a mind of their own.

'W-what are you doing?' she croaked as his head started to come down.

'I'm going to kiss you.'

'I t-told you not to touch me.' *Damn!* she thought. That hadn't sounded half as strident as she'd intended.

'I know you did but Jim and Pearl could be watching from the house,' he said.

She stared at his mouth, her heart leaping at the thought of feeling his lips and tongue playing with hers. 'It's a long way to the house. They couldn't possibly see us from here…you don't have to kiss me…'

'Perhaps not, but I thought I might do so all the same.'

'I—I don't want you to kiss me unless it's absolutely necessary.'

'Oh, it's necessary, all right,' he said, brushing her lips with his in a light-as-air movement that set her mouth tingling. 'It's absolutely necessary.'

Hayley sighed as he swooped back down and covered her mouth with his, his tongue driving through the shield of her lips in search of hers. Her lower body jumped in response, her breasts swelling against his chest as he used one hand on the small of her back to bring her closer. She felt the intoxicating heat of his erection and marvelled that his blood had surged so quickly in reaction to her closeness. It gave her a sense of feminine power that her body was exciting to him, especially when he had spurned her clumsy adolescent advances all those years ago.

The skin of his jaw rasped her face as he deepened the kiss with an urgency that thrilled her. She felt her lips swelling beneath the demanding pressure of his, her whole body quivering to feel more and more of his touch. The dew of arousal budded between her legs, her tail bone tilting in delight as his fingers explored each small knob of her vertebrae. She pushed herself closer, her achingly empty heated core searching for his thickness to fill it with throbbing, exhilarating life.

His tongue swept the cavern of her mouth once more, flicking against hers in a provocative caress that fuelled her need of him like a match to a live gas outlet. The combustion of his touch as his hands moved to her breasts to cup them sent her over the edge of reason and control.

She fumbled between them for the zipper on his jeans, her fingers relishing in the spring of his engorged flesh as she finally freed him. She heard him groan deep in the back of his throat, but he did nothing to stop her as she explored him with a touch at first tentative, then increasingly bold as she felt his tightly reined in response. He felt like satin-wrapped steel under the soft pads of her fingertips, the sticky moistness at the tip bringing her gaze down to look at him in awe. He was much bigger than she'd expected, and uncut, which made him seem all the more primal and dangerous.

'You're going to have stop doing that, right now,' he said on a harshly indrawn breath. 'Otherwise I won't be held responsible for my actions.'

She kept stroking him, but he snatched at her hand, his fingers around hers almost painfully tight as they pulled her off him.

'No, Hayley,' he said, breathing hard. 'This is taking things way too far.'

Hayley felt her face fire up and mentally kicked herself for revealing how much he affected her.

She gave her head a little toss. 'If you think you can kiss me whenever you like you need to realise I can do the same to you. That's fair, isn't it?'

'Kissing is one thing but stimulating me to—'

'You could have stopped me earlier,' she cut him off. 'Why didn't you?'

He looked down at her for several pulsing seconds, his expression like a mask. 'God knows,' he said and, turning away, began to stride towards the river.

Hayley let out a painful sigh and followed a few paces behind, her legs dragging against the weight of the long grass.

She caught up to him a short time later and came to stand beside him as he looked out over the river to the blue-tinged hills beyond.

'Are you really going to keep this place?' she asked.

He glanced at her briefly. 'You don't think I'd look good in a pair of moleskins and elastic-sided work boots?'

'I don't know. Can you ride a horse?'

'No, but I can ride a quad bike. At least they don't bite and kick.'

'But they can still be dangerous,' she said. 'Several people have been killed on the land using them.'

'Well, if I am you can collect my life insurance. That should set you up for life.'

'Don't joke about stuff like that,' she said, frowning at him in reproach.

His dark eyes came back to hers. 'Why? Would you miss fighting with me?'

Hayley wanted to say she'd miss everything about him: the melted chocolate of his eyes, his teasing smile, his electric touch and his too tempting mouth and body.

'Maybe,' she acceded, beginning to walk back the way they had come.

She felt his shoulder brush against hers and tried to move further away, but she almost lost her footing on the uneven ground.

'Careful,' he said and steadied her.

She looked up at him. 'We've always fought, though, haven't we?' she said. 'From the first moment we met we were at each other's throats.'

'Yeah, pretty much, I guess.'

'Why do you think that was?' she asked.

His mouth tilted into a teasing grin. 'Well for one thing you could have written and proofread the textbook on being spoilt.'

She gave him a thump on the arm. 'And you were a surly teenager who thought it was beneath you to speak to a little kid five years younger.'

'It seemed a big gap back then, didn't it?' he commented as they wandered on. 'I mean, you were fourteen and I was nineteen when my father married your mother. That's a whole different ball game from now. I'm thirty-three and you're twenty-eight. Those five years have shrunk a lot.'

They walked a few more paces in silence. Hayley watched as Jasper absently snapped off a strand of long grass and threaded it through his fingers. His expression was clouded, as if he was thinking about his parent's divorce and how her mother Eva had ruined so many lives. There was a shadow of something in his dark eyes as they looked into the distance. He reminded her of a lone wolf on a mountain top, surveying his territory.

He suddenly turned and looked down at her. 'Have you ever wondered who your father was?' he asked.

Hayley shifted her gaze so he wouldn't see how ashamed

she was of her background. She had longed to find out in the early years, but after her mother had hinted the one she suspected was responsible was now behind bars serving time for a serious crime she had left the subject well alone. 'No...' she answered.

Jasper took her hand in his as they came into closer view of the homestead, his forehead lined with a frown. 'I guess sometimes in life there might be worse things than growing up without knowing who your real father is.'

'Like being forced to marry your stepsister?' she asked as she fell into step beside him.

His fingers tightened momentarily around hers as if her words had annoyed him. 'Being married to anyone wasn't in my immediate plans for my life, but I'm sure I'll get used to it.'

'It's only temporary.' She hated that her tone sounded a little piqued, but she just couldn't help it.

'Yeah,' he said. 'It's only temporary.'

'And I bet you can't wait for it to be over,' she said, still unable to remove the edge of resentment in her voice.

'Actually,' he said with a satirical glint in his dark eyes as he swung his gaze back down to hers, 'if what happened back down there by the river is any indication of what our marriage is going to be like, I can't wait for it to start.'

CHAPTER SEVEN

HAYLEY KNEW HER cheeks were blazing, but there was little she could do to control it. 'It won't happen again,' she said stiffly.

'Pity.'

'You said we weren't going to have a real marriage. A hands off arrangement, wasn't that what you said?' she asked, her heart beginning to race as Jasper's dark gaze meshed with hers.

'We could have a rethink on that. I like the feel of your hands.'

She turned away from his tempting gaze. 'I don't want to sleep with you.'

'You have a very unique way of communicating that,' he quipped.

She tried to pull her hand from his but he wouldn't allow it. 'You promised you'd be celibate for the duration of our marriage,' she said.

'I took that to mean I wasn't to sleep with other women,' he said. 'It doesn't mean I can't sleep with you if that's what you want.'

'Well, I don't want it.' *Liar!* a little voice sounded in her head.

She began to walk on but he swung her around to face him,

tipping up her chin with a very strong finger. 'You've wanted me since you were sixteen years old, sugar, but back then I was too much of a gentleman to take what was on offer. You were half tanked and would have regretted it the next morning.'

'You're hardly what I'd call a gentleman now,' she flashed back. 'You're ruthless, shallow, self-serving and...and...selfish.'

He grinned at her devilishly. 'You left out sexy.'

She set her mouth in a prim line. 'I don't find you the least bit sexy.'

'Yes you do,' he drawled as he rubbed the pad of his thumb over her bottom lip. 'If I hadn't stopped you, you were going to put that pouting little mouth around me and suck me dry, weren't you?'

Hayley's belly exploded with desire. She felt the hot flash of it hit her from above and below, coming to a scorching, bubbling pool of liquid fire between her thighs. Her breasts tingled and her mouth quivered under the sensuous stroke of his thumb. She felt the most irresistible urge to draw it into her mouth and suck on it, hard, as she had wanted to do to him down by the river.

Everything about him made her feel reckless and out of control. The challenging gleam in his eyes made it a thousand times worse. She wanted to pull him down to the grass at their feet and run her hands all over him, to explore his sculptured muscles, to taste the sexy saltiness of his skin, to taste the essence of what made him a man.

She pulled her shoulders back to keep her breasts away from his chest but instead it pushed her pelvis into intimate contact with his. 'Let me go.' She somehow got her voice to work in spite of her shallow, erratic breathing. 'Please...'

He placed his hands on her bottom and held her tight against him, the jut of his erection making her gasp involuntarily. His eyes burned into the wide ocean blue-green of hers, his chest rising and falling against the soft press of her breasts.

'No, I don't think so,' he said, his voice sounding deep and gravelly as it rumbled against her chest.

'Jasper…*please,*' she pleaded. 'The Hendersons are probably watching us.'

'And no doubt thinking we can't wait to get married next weekend,' he said, gazing down at the softness of her mouth.

Hayley's belly did another flip flop at the thought that this time next week they would have been married twenty-four hours.

He brought his mouth down and branded hers with a swift hard kiss before releasing her. She swayed on her feet for a millisecond, feeling disoriented and unfocussed.

'Come on, baby girl.' He took her arm and tucked it under his, the corners of his mouth tilting wryly. 'You're even starting to convince *me* you're in love with me. Now there's a scary thought.'

Hayley racked her brain for something pithy to say, but for the life of her couldn't think of a single thing. She trudged beside him with uncharacteristic meekness, her teeth doing serious damage to her bottom lip all the way back to the house.

After Jasper had seen to the business side of things, the Hendersons insisted Hayley and he stay for lunch. Hayley would have preferred leaving so she could cut short her performance as the besotted fiancée, but she could see how keen Pearl was for company, especially as her husband was so sadly disabled.

Hayley sat beside Jim during the meal and cut up his meat and salad so he could eat with one hand using a fork. He gave her a lopsided smile of gratefulness and mumbled his thanks.

Once or twice during the meal she looked up to find Jasper's chocolate-brown gaze resting on her. Conscious of the elderly couple sitting watching, Hayley had no choice but to send him a small smile each time.

'It takes you back, doesn't it, love?' Pearl asked Jim with a dreamy sigh. 'Remember when we were first engaged and married? We couldn't bear to look at anyone else but each other.'

Jim's eyes twinkled at his wife.

'How did you meet?' Hayley asked, hoping to divert the attention from her relationship with Jasper.

'Jim was a couple of years ahead of me at school,' Pearl said. 'He used to pull my pigtails during recess. I hated him for most of my childhood and teenage years, but one day a few years later he came to visit my father about some stock he wanted to buy, but I kept in the background. He kept coming back week after week until he'd bought so many sheep my father started to suspect something. The next time Jim came around Dad sent me out and that was it. I fell in love with him on the spot.'

'That's *so* romantic,' Hayley said, caught up in the magic of it all. 'I would love to have a man so in love with me…' She suddenly faltered as she realised what she had almost revealed. 'I mean, I never imagined I would have the same thing happen to me…but it did…sort of…'

Pearl smiled. 'Jasper told us how you lived in the same house since you were fourteen,' she said. 'When did you suddenly realise he was the one?'

'Um…I pretty much knew it since I was about sixteen,' she said, carefully avoiding Jasper's eyes.

'That's funny.' Pearl's brows snuggled together momentarily. 'I thought Jasper said you were engaged to someone else but he swept you off your feet right at the last minute.'

'Um…er…yes…' Hayley felt her cheeks fire up again. 'I was engaged to someone else. Silly, really, when you think of it. I should have been more patient. I should have known Jasper would come round in the end.'

'Just as well he did,' Pearl remarked soberly. 'Think of how dreadful it would have been if you had married the other man when you were really in love with Jasper.'

'Dreadful,' Hayley agreed, nodding her head in agreement. 'I can't bear to even think about it.'

'I hope you're not going to put off having a family like so many young women these days,' Pearl said. 'I know several women who left it too late.'

'Oh, no, of course not,' Hayley said, watching Jasper begin to squirm in his chair. She realised she was starting to enjoy herself now that her little vocal slip had gone by unnoticed. 'We want to start straight away and have at least three, don't we, darling?'

'That's right, sweetheart,' he said, his dark eyes flashing an unmistakable warning that sent a lightning bolt between her legs. 'But I want you all to myself for a little while yet.'

'And a dog,' Hayley added hastily, her colour still high. 'Maybe even two, but not those little handbag-size yappy ones. Something…er…bigger.'

Pearl sat back with an indulgent smile. 'I can see you two are going to be very happy together. It seems like a match made in heaven.'

'It is,' Hayley said brightly. *But it's going to be hell on the way home,* she added under her breath when she caught the look in Jasper's eyes as she rose to help clear the table.

She was right.

They had barely traversed the driveway before he turned a blistering glance her way. 'What the hell were you playing at back there?' he asked.

'Nothing.'

'Nothing be damned,' he growled. 'You nearly lifted the lid on our charade. For God's sake, Hayley, watch your big mouth.'

'*My* big mouth?' She tossed him a heated glare. 'I didn't know what lies you'd already told them about us. How was I to know what to say?'

'That stuff about kids was totally uncalled for,' he bit out. 'You know what I think about kids.'

'You don't like kids?'

'I like them but I don't want them.'

She sent him an ironic look. 'What a pity that is, for you already have one, or have you conveniently forgotten all about Daniel Moorebank? How old is he now? Fourteen? Fifteen?'

Hayley couldn't help noticing the suddenly harsh set of his features, his mouth tightened to the point of whiteness and his dark angry gaze fixed on the road ahead. 'He's fifteen.'

'Do you ever see him?'

'Occasionally.'

'But you don't want more children in your life.'

'No.'

'Are you close to Daniel?' she asked.

'He's a good kid,' Jasper said, keeping his eyes straight ahead. 'But I can't be the father he wants. I'm not prepared to risk it with anyone else.'

'That's a totally selfish way of looking at it,' she said. 'What about if the woman you're involved with on a more permanent basis some time in the future wants children? It's not fair to rob her of that chance.'

'I'm not planning on anything permanent.'

She folded her arms crossly. 'You really are as shallow and selfish as the press makes out. Do you realise there are numerous women out there who are circumstantially childless because they happened to fall in love with selfish men like you?'

'I've always been up front with the women in my life about the issue of children,' Jasper said. 'I always wear a condom. I don't want to find myself in the same position as...' he cleared his throat and hoped she wouldn't notice his slight hesitation '…I found myself when I was eighteen.'

She gaped at him. 'You really are serious about this, aren't you?'

'Are you currently on oral contraception?'

She tossed her hair over one shoulder huffily. 'That's none of your business.'

'I have a feeling that this time next week it will be.'

She gave her eyes an exaggerated roll. 'You must be joking.'

'If you have any ideas of tricking me into a permanent role in your life, then get rid of them right now,' he said. 'As far as I'm concerned this is a one-act play and then the curtain is coming down.'

'Fine by me.'

'And I would advise against financial paybacks,' he said. 'I know that's the way most women like to play it, your mother being a pertinent example, but I will make sure you are adequately compensated without you having to strip me of half my wealth. I haven't worked my butt off for the last fifteen years to have you come along and sweep it from under me like your mother did to my father.'

'You know, you have some really serious trust issues with women,' she observed. 'You really should see someone about it.'

'What I have is a healthy dose of cynicism,' he countered. 'Even the strongest marriages can collapse. My parents were happy until your mother came waltzing in and lured him away with her come-to-bed eyes and body.'

'That's funny,' she threw back. 'You told me that if a man *really* loved a woman nothing and no one would be able to lure him away from her. Have you suddenly changed your mind or did you just say that to make sure I didn't forgive Myles and marry him regardless?'

'No, I didn't just say that,' he said, frowning slightly. 'My father regretted his relationship with your mother. I know he did but he was too proud to admit it to me. He didn't want to hear me say I told you so. He spoke to Raymond about it, however, knowing of course that my brother would forgive him in accordance with his beliefs.'

'But you can't forgive him, can you?' she asked, looking at him again. 'You can never forgive him for hurting your mother.'

His jaw tensed. 'No, that I can never forgive.'

'And you can never quite forgive me for being her daughter, can you?' she said in a small thin voice.

Jasper glanced at her briefly, his chest feeling as if someone had it in a vice when he saw the flicker of pain in her blue-green eyes. He turned back to the road, wishing he could find the words to take away the bitterness of the past. He envied his brother, who could find it in himself to forgive even the worst of sins. But then Raymond was a bigger and better person than he was. He had already done so much good in the community, his love and sacrifice healing those damaged by the selfishness of others, which was even more reason why Jasper had to keep Hayley away from the truth about Daniel Moorebank.

'I've perhaps been unnecessarily hard on you for something you had no control over,' he said at last. 'We can't choose our parents. We get what we get and have to make the most of it.'

'I would have liked to have had a father,' she said after another tiny silence. 'I guess that's why I clung to Gerald such a lot…he filled an emptiness in my life.'

He looked at her again. 'So what you're saying is you've been carrying around a dad-shaped hole all your life.'

Her chest deflated on a little sigh. 'Yes…I guess that is what I'm saying.'

Silence again.

'Do you think that's why you rushed into your relationship with Myles Lederman?' he asked, 'Because you were searching for another father-figure?'

'I don't know…' She released another sigh. 'Maybe. Lucy, my friend at the salon seemed to think so. I just want to be happy. I want a family to call my own. I want it all.'

'You can't have it all,' he said. 'No one can, or at least not for ever.'

'But what about the Hendersons?' she asked. 'They still love each other after all these years. That's what I want.'

'You want an old man dribbling in a wheelchair some time in your future, do you?'

She gave him a reproving look. 'He was once a strong, fit man like you. Pearl loves him for who he is as a person. That's real love, Jasper. That's what I want.'

He shook his head in disbelief. 'You really need to see someone about that idealistic complex you have. The world isn't full of happy ever afters, Hayley. You of all people should know that.'

'I know life isn't always perfect, but I want my kids to have a different life from mine.' She clamped down on her lip and then releasing it, confessed, 'I hated my childhood. The constant stream of horrible men who came and went. I hated changing schools all the time. I hated being the odd one out, the one with the worst clothes while my mother wore the latest fashions. I hated all of it. No child should have to go through that and no child of mine will. I swear to God I won't let it happen.'

Jasper frowned at the bitterness in her tone. 'I hadn't realised you were so unhappy. You seemed to enjoy living at Crickglades.'

'I did,' she said. 'It was the first real home we'd ever lived in.' She let out a little sigh and added, 'We'd always lived in flats or council houses. Crickglades was the first real garden I'd ever been able to wander about in. I used to love the roses. There were so many of them and when it was hot the scent of them would fill the air. I loved that.'

He swallowed against the walnut-sized lump of emotion blocking his throat. How like his mother she had sounded!

'I hated leaving when Gerald divorced my mother,' she said in the same soft tone. 'He asked me to stay but I thought it would upset you too much.'

He reached over and took her hand and gave it a tiny squeeze. 'You were just a kid, sweetheart. A rather cute kid, if I remember correctly.'

She sent him an ironic look. 'I thought you said I was a spoilt brat?'

'You were.'

She pulled her hand out of his and pouted at him. 'You can never hand out a compliment without a sting in its tail somewhere, can you?'

He smiled at her before turning back to the road. 'Just keeping you in your place, baby girl. I don't want you to get a big head just because you're the only woman who has managed so far to get me within a bull's roar of an altar.'

'We're not there yet,' she said with a defiant hitch of her chin. 'I could always pull the plug, even now at this late stage.'

His dark eyes glinted at her meaningfully. 'You could indeed, but then that would be asking for trouble, now, wouldn't it?'

She settled back in her seat with a scowl. 'It seems to me I'm going to be knee deep in trouble no matter what I do.'

'Only knee deep, huh?' he mused as he took an exit leading her to flat. 'I was thinking a little higher than that.'

CHAPTER EIGHT

As soon as Jasper turned into her street Hayley saw the SOLD sign on the building where her one bedroom ground-floor flat was situated. She stared at it in shock for several heart-chugging seconds before turning to look at him. 'Let me guess,' she said with an accusing glare. 'You're my new landlord here too, right?'

He gave her a smug smile. 'That's right, sugar.'

She gritted her teeth and flung open the car door, slamming it behind her forcefully. She began stomping towards the building, her back and shoulders stiff with fury.

'I just had to buy it. It was going for a song,' he said, catching up to her with ease.

She threw him a castigating look over one shoulder. 'I just bet it was.'

'It was,' he said. 'It's got great development potential too. You know what they say about the three big selling points: location, location, location.'

She turned to face him once they were inside, her hands on her hips. 'That's funny, but my landlady didn't mention a thing about putting it on the market.'

He gave her a guileless look. 'She must have forgotten to mention it to you.'

'Why are you doing this?' she asked, frowning at him heavily.

'I'm just making sure you don't change your mind at the last minute,' he said. 'I'll be away on business for most of this week so I can't afford to have you pulling out of the deal while my back is turned. Call it insurance, if you like.'

She clenched her teeth as she glared at him. 'It's blackmail, that's what it is.'

He lifted one shoulder up and down indifferently before reaching for a piece of paper inside his pocket. He handed it to her with a hint of a smile in his dark eyes. 'I took the liberty of depositing funds into your bank account to cover the expenses of the wedding and honeymoon you'd already paid for. If you think that's not enough let me know and I'll reimburse you further.'

Hayley took the deposit slip from him, her fingers briefly touching his. 'Thank you.'

'Fair's fair,' he said. 'You're only marrying me because I've insisted on it. It's only right that I pay for all the expenses incurred.'

'Maybe…but it seems such a waste of money going on a honeymoon neither of us wants.'

A small silence dilated the atmosphere until Hayley could feel the temptation of forbidden opportunities closing in on her. A vision of their straining bodies locked in passion flitted unbidden into her mind, and her cheeks grew hot, her heart starting to thump so loudly she was surprised he couldn't hear it.

He closed the distance between them in one stride and tipped up her chin with the tip of his finger. 'Then I'd better make sure not a minute of it goes to waste,' he said, his eyes burning with sexual promise.

Hayley stepped backwards out of his hold with what little resistance she had left and kept her features deceptively composed. 'Do me a favour, Jasper, and keep your hands to yourself,' she said coldly.

'I can read your body,' he said. 'And yours keeps telling me it wants me.'

'You're imagining it.'

His eyes glinted teasingly. 'So I was imagining those soft little pads of your fingertips running up and down me earlier today, was I?'

She drew herself up rigidly, her face and body feeling as if a bush fire had been let loose inside. 'I won't be so foolish as to let myself get carried away again by thinking one man can substitute another.'

By way of response he stepped forward and, taking her head in both his hands, he bent down and kissed her hard on the mouth. 'See you in church, baby girl.'

The days leading to the wedding began to go by so quickly Hayley had little time to think of any last-minute escape routes, even if by some slim chance Jasper had overlooked one she could have executed. A small part of her had more or less accepted her fate with fatalistic resignation, while another part—a much larger part—began embracing it not only willingly but with increasing fervour as each day passed. The sexual tension she felt each time she was with Jasper had increased in intensity to the point where she could barely look him in the eyes without imagining he could see how she felt. The simplest touch of his hand or shoulder as he moved past her had her body tingling with awareness, and when his gaze locked with hers she felt her stomach roll over in heady anticipation of experiencing the full extent of the attraction she could see reflected in his dark chocolate eyes. That their short marriage would remain unconsummated was becoming increasingly unlikely, and, while Hayley realised Jasper would very likely move on once the month was up without a single qualm, she knew that for her things would never be the same. Her harmless adolescent crush had matured into something much more imminently dangerous…

* * *

The day before the ceremony Lucy announced another visitor at the salon. 'And, no, it's neither Myles nor Jasper,' she said in response to Hayley's questioning expression. 'It's a priest.'

Hayley felt her shoulders instantly relax. 'It's Raymond, Jasper's older brother.'

Lucy's eyes went wide. 'Jasper's brother is a *priest*? Wow! A playboy and a celibate priest in the one family. That's certainly going from one extreme to another.'

Hayley gave her a tell-me-about-it look and went out to Reception where Raymond was standing looking like a fish that had just been tipped out of its aquarium.

She'd lately felt a little awkward in his company since he'd taken his final orders; she didn't know whether it was appropriate to give him a hug or kiss on the cheek. Instead she offered her hand and he took it briefly, but warmly.

'Hello, Hayley,' he said. 'I hope you don't mind me coming to see you without making an appointment.'

'You don't have to make an appointment to see me, Raymond.' She smiled and in an attempt at humour added, 'That is unless you want a manicure or something.'

His answering smile looked a little strained around the edges. 'Is there somewhere we can talk in private?' he asked.

'Of course,' she said, and led him out to her shoebox size office.

She watched as he sat in the seat she offered, silently measuring the differences she could see between him and Jasper. Although they were brothers there was little to identify them as such. While Jasper's hair was dark and thick, Raymond's was several shades lighter and even though he was only four years older than Jasper, the stealthy creep of baldness was very apparent. His skin too was lighter and failed to catch and keep the kiss of the sun they way Jasper's did.

He took the seat she offered and drew in a preparatory breath before speaking. 'I will come straight to the point, Hayley. I have some grave concerns about your marriage to Jasper tomorrow. I really don't think you should go through with it.'

She waited a beat or two before responding. 'What are your main objections?'

'I love my brother very dearly, but there's no escaping the fact that he's using you to make himself a fortune he doesn't need,' he said. 'And you are aiding and abetting him.'

'You make it sound like a crime.'

'It *is* a crime to tie yourself to a man who will only use you for his own purposes,' he said. 'I hate saying this about my own flesh and blood, but Jasper has an edge of ruthlessness about him. I'm worried about you, Hayley,' he said. 'Jasper made your time at Crickglades a misery. You were always crying about something he'd said or done. How much worse might it be being married to him?'

Hayley felt a frown tug at her brows. 'For G…er…I mean Pete's sake, Raymond, I was a pimply teenager with hormones going up and down. Anyone could have made me cry at the drop of a hat. I don't think Jasper meant anything by it. He was hurting too; I was just too young to see it at the time.'

His inspection of her features was speculative. 'You sound as if you really like him now. I thought you hated him.'

She gave him an ironic look. 'I thought you of all people would have been encouraging me to put aside such destructive feelings and work on forgiveness.'

'Perhaps you're right, but I still feel it's my responsibility to warn you of what you are getting yourself into,' he said. 'You realise that in the eyes of the church your marriage will be considered eternal and sacred?'

'Listen, Raymond.' She leaned forward so she could eyeball him. 'I consider what I *feel* for Jasper to be eternal and sacred.

I don't care what the church has to say about it. As far as I'm concerned it's between him and me.'

'God help you,' he said, getting to his feet. 'You've fallen in love with him.'

'No. I don't love him, but I don't hate him as I did when we were growing up,' she confessed.

'And you think you can reform him, do you?' His tone contained an element of frustration. 'Do you know how many women I counsel in my parish who for years have foolishly thought they could reform the men in their lives? There are some men for whom no amount of love is enough, and I'm very much afraid Jasper might turn out to be one of them. He's stubborn and finds it impossible to forgive. How long do you think such a marriage will last?'

'I guess I'll just have to pray for a miracle, then,' she said.

He let out a long-winded sigh and got to his feet. 'You'll need more than a miracle.' He took both her hands in his and gave them a comforting squeeze. 'If you ever need someone to help you, I will be there for you, Hayley. Please remember that.'

Tears pricked at her eyes at the tender and sincere concern she could see reflected in his. 'Thank you, Raymond. I will remember that.'

He dropped her hands and let out another regretful sigh. 'I'm sorry I couldn't be there for you tomorrow. Jasper did ask me but I already have another wedding on.'

'It's all right, Raymond. Knowing you'll be thinking of me will be enough.'

He smiled sadly and reached for the door. 'I hope that you get your miracle, Hayley,' he said. 'I will be praying for you.'

'Thanks,' she said. 'I think I'm going to need all the help I can get.'

* * *

Hayley stood on the portal of the church on Saturday morning with Lucy fluttering about her like a moth around a very bright light.

'Are you ready?' Lucy asked as she gave Hayley's veil one final tweak.

She drew in a long steadying breath. 'I think so.'

'Righto, let's go, then.'

As soon as Hayley met Jasper's eyes as she began to walk towards him she felt something sharp catch in her chest. She saw the sudden flare of his dark gaze, the slightly shell-shocked expression that briefly marked his features before he got it under control as she came to stand beside him.

He looked down at her through the gossamer of her veil and smiled. 'You look very beautiful.'

She smiled back, conscious of the indulgent congregation watching them. 'You look rather good yourself,' she said, although she couldn't help noticing he looked a little pale beneath his tan.

The priest began the service and Hayley was swept up in the exchanging of vows, her voice trembling slightly over the words as she realised how deeply she meant the promises she was making. Jasper's voice wasn't as convincing as hers, she noted with a flood of resentment, and when he leaned down to kiss her it was hardly what she would have called enthusiastic.

Once the register was signed they made their way back down the aisle and into the sunshine and the array of photographers all pressing forward for the perfect shot.

The reception soon followed and after a couple of glasses of champagne Hayley tried to fool herself into believing every part of the day was for real and for ever. There was no other way to survive it without bursting into tears of despair.

Jasper was silent for most of the time. His one-word responses to the questions some of the guests fired at him made Hayley brood with anger that he had insisted on her playing the part of the besotted bride while he moped about looking as if his life had suddenly come to an end.

Finally it was over and Jasper escorted her to the limousine he had waiting. She sat stiffly in the seat once they had left the cheering guests behind and sent him a blistering glance. 'Well, thanks for making me look a complete idiot back there,' she said crossly.

He loosened his tie as if it were suddenly choking him. 'What are you talking about?' he asked.

'You could have at least sounded and acted like you were enjoying yourself. Half the time you looked as if someone had a gun pressed to your head.'

'Yeah, well, that's what it felt like,' Jasper remarked with a wry grimace as he rubbed at his temple where a bullet-hole of pain was boring into his skull. 'It was a big week, a lot to organise.'

Hayley could just imagine what sort of mischief he had got up to on his so-called business trip. He hadn't even told her where he'd gone. 'How was your business trip?' she asked, feigning an interest she wasn't sure she really felt.

He leaned his head back against the seat and closed his eyes. 'You don't have to play the loving bride now, Hayley; no one's watching.'

She frowned at his tone. 'There's no need to be so rude. I was only trying to make conversation.'

'I have the mother of all headaches, if you must know,' he said, opening one eye to look at her. 'I just need a couple of hours of sleep and I'll be back on my feet.'

'You should have told me.' She gave him a suddenly contrite look. 'We could have left much earlier.'

He waved her concern away with a flick of his hand as he closed his eyes again. 'I'll be fine.'

But he wasn't, Hayley realised as soon as they arrived at his house a short time later. His features had turned a ghastly shade of grey and his legs gave a distinct wobble as he got out of the car.

'You don't look so good,' she said, taking his arm.

He removed her hand and began to walk towards the house but within a couple of metres his legs gave way and he stumbled to his knees.

Hayley rushed to his aid but he brushed her off with an irritated growl. 'Leave me alone. You'll get your dress filthy.'

'I don't care a thing about my dress,' she said, and grabbed his elbow and hauled him to his feet with a strength she'd had no idea she possessed. 'I'm taking you to bed right this minute.'

He looked at her through bloodshot eyes. 'What a time to tell me that,' he said with a rueful twist to his mouth.

She rolled her eyes and half led, half lugged him to the front door, putting her arm around his waist.

'You're not going to carry me over the threshold, are you?' he asked, swaying on his feet. 'That's supposed to be my job.'

'If I have to I will,' she said and proceeded to drag him through to the nearest bathroom.

He sagged against the toiilet, his face ashen. 'You can go out now,' he groaned.

'You must be joking,' she said, reaching for a towel and dampening it at the basin. 'This is no time for modesty, Jasper. You've obviously picked up some sort of nasty bug.'

'Which you will catch if you come near me.'

She ignored his hand as he held it to ward her off and pressed the folded towel to the back of his neck. 'You're burning like a furnace,' she said. 'I think I should call a doctor.'

'Don't you dare.' He gripped the edge of the bath to drag

himself upright and, taking the towel off her, buried his face into its cool dampness.

Hayley bit her lip in concern. 'Jasper, I've never seen you ill before. What if it's serious? Like appendicitis or something?'

'I told you I'm fine. It's just a headache.'

'It must be a migraine,' she said.

'I've never had one before…'

She reached up and helped him out of his jacket and to her surprise he didn't resist. She undid his tie and shirt as well, but his hands came down over hers when she reached for the waistband of his trousers.

'Not tonight, sweetheart,' he said with another attempt at a wry smile. 'I'm not feeling up to it, so to speak.'

She shook her head at him reprovingly and asked, 'Will you be OK in the shower? I'll wait just outside in case you need me.'

'Give me ten minutes,' he said. 'Then if you don't get an answer ring my insurance broker and tell him you'll be in to collect my life insurance in the morning. It should set you up for life.'

She tightened her mouth. 'Sometimes you can be such a jerk,' she said. 'I didn't marry you for your money and you damn well know it.'

'Why did you marry me, Hayley?'

'You know why.'

Jasper's eyes fell away from hers as he reached for the shower door. 'Yeah,' he said, leaning his burning head against the cold pane of glass for a moment. 'I blackmailed you into it, right?'

But when he opened his eyes to see why she hadn't answered she had already gone.

CHAPTER NINE

HAYLEY WENT INTO Jasper's room to pull back the covers of his bed when her eyes came upon the suitcase he had packed in preparation for their flight the next morning. Her own suitcase as well as her belongings had been picked up that morning by one of his staff and brought to the house and placed in one of the spare rooms.

She turned down the covers of the bed and closed the curtains just as Jasper came in with a towel wrapped around his waist. He was still looking as white as the sheets on his bed, his features looking even more chiselled than normal, sharpened by illness.

'What will we do about tomorrow?' she asked as he sat down heavily on the bed. 'Do you think we should cancel?'

He lifted his weary gaze to hers. 'We don't leave until lunch-time, but would you be disappointed if we did?'

'Of course not. You're hardly well enough to go up and down the stairs let alone fly to a tropical island.' She touched him on the forehead with the flat of her palm. 'You're still running a fever. I'll get you something to bring it down.'

When she came back with some paracetamol and a glass of water he was lying in the bed, the towel he had been wearing tossed on the floor. She sat on the edge of the bed, conscious of his naked body lying with just a sheet of Egyptian cotton separating her from him.

'Here you go,' she said, handing him the tablets.

'Thanks.' He tipped back his head and swallowed them with a mouthful of water.

'Can I get you anything else?' she asked.

'No.'

'Are you sure?'

He opened one eye to look at her. 'Please go away, Hayley. You don't have to worry. I'm not going to hold you to that in-sickness-and-health routine.'

She screwed up her mouth at him and got up from the bed. 'I'll leave the door open so if you need me you can call out. I'll move my things into the spare room next door.'

'You'd be better to stay as far away as possible in case it's contagious.'

'It's probably too late for caution,' she said. 'You kissed me, don't forget. Not that it was a very good kiss or anything.'

'I didn't want to pass on my germs.'

'You should have told me you weren't feeling well,' she said with a little nibble of her bottom lip.

He cracked one eye open again. 'What would that have achieved? The church was full of guests, the caterers had prepared the reception food and drinks and the press were jostling about like ants at a picnic.'

Hayley sighed as she gave the bed another quick straighten. 'Are you sure about the doctor? I can ring a twenty-four-hour clinic if you like.'

He opened both of his eyes this time to send her a hardened glare. 'You seem to be having a bit of a problem right now understanding the word no.'

She gave him an arch look in return. 'Yes, well, I've heard it said that married couples often end up very similar, perhaps it's a trait that's brushed off on me from you already.'

He closed his eyes again on a sigh of defeat. 'Give me a break, sweetheart. Don't kick me when I'm already down.'

Hayley felt totally disarmed by his uncharacteristic vulnerability, all her nurturing tendencies coming to the fore. She came back to his side and stroked his burning forehead again, her touch gentle and soothing. 'I'm sorry,' she said in a soft whisper.

He touched the back of her hand briefly with one of his. 'Be a good little girl and let me ride this out alone. I'm not used to having anyone fussing over me.'

'You don't have to be alone,' she said, but if he heard her he gave no indication of it. She watched his chest rising and falling, his breathing pattern evening out until finally she felt his body relax as he drifted off to sleep.

Hayley checked on him three times before she went to bed herself, but each time he seemed to be sleeping soundly. She had transferred her things to the room closest to his and, after spending a short time unpacking, she looked longingly at the bed. She had been up early and, with the added stress of pretending she was pretending to be in love, she felt as if every bit of energy had drained out of her completely.

She was furious with herself for being so weak. How could she have fallen in love with him knowing him as she did? He was the last person who could give her what she wanted in life. He had already ruined one woman's life, abandoning his own son to pursue a playboy lifestyle free of commitments.

She got into bed and closed her eyes, willing herself to sleep so she didn't have to think about the way his mouth had felt on hers...

She woke some hours later to the sound of Jasper being wretchedly sick in the *en suite*. She hesitated, torn between wanting to go to him, but realising he wanted to be left alone to maintain some level of dignity.

She couldn't remember a time in the past when he'd been so ill. Even the common colds that had knocked her flat occasionally during her childhood and adolescent years had seemed to pass him by with little or no effect. She wondered if he'd taught himself self sufficiency from an early age due to the loss of his mother. He reminded her of a wolf licking his wounds in private, unwilling to show his physical vulnerability in case someone took advantage of it.

Deciding it was better to check than lie awake worrying about him, she put a wrap on over her nightgown and pressed her ear to the door of his room. 'Jasper? Are you OK?'

It was disturbingly quiet.

She turned the handle and entered the bedroom, her eyes immediately taking in the twisted sheets, which looked damp with sweat.

The *en suite* door was slightly ajar and when she pushed it open she found Jasper slumped between the basin and the toilet, his face ashen.

'Oh, you poor thing,' she said, rushing to him. 'Have you hurt yourself?'

'I'm all right…' he groaned, and tried to lift his head but gave up and let it drop to the tiles once more.

'That's it,' she said. 'I'm calling a doctor.'

'While you're at it you might as well call the undertaker as well,' he said dryly as he closed his eyes against the light.

She rinsed out a face cloth and gently bathed his face and, leaving him propped up with towels and some pillows from the bed, went to the phone.

The medical clinic promised someone would be there within half an hour and she went back to him in time to see him struggling to stand upright.

She felt her bottom lip begin to quiver and tears pushed past her eyelids even though she blinked and squeezed several times to stop them.

Jasper dragged his blurry gaze to the source of the moisture that was dripping on his arm. 'Please tell me those aren't tears of joy at the thought of me meeting my demise,' he said with a touch of irony.

She gulped back a sob. 'I can't bear to see you like this. I can't bear to see anyone like this.'

'I must look a whole lot worse than I feel, which is really saying something because I feel like a headstone with my name on it is hammering me over the head.'

'The doctor is on his way or her way—I don't know which; the receptionist didn't say.' She sniffed and wiped away her tears with the back of her hand.

Jasper felt a small smile tug at his mouth in spite of how he felt. 'You're starting to really scare me with all this wifely concern, baby girl. A guy could get used to it.'

Her big blue-green eyes met his, her small chin wobbling as she tried to return his smile. 'We could go on one of those reality TV shows, you know—honeymoons from hell or something,' she said. 'I think we'd win.'

'You could be right.'

The doorbell sounded and she sprang to her feet. 'That'll be the doctor.'

He watched as she raced out, his throat feeling as if he'd swallowed a thorn and it was now on its way down his windpipe to his chest, catching him now and again. He hadn't realised how much he missed being fussed over until now. He had shut down his emotions after his mother's death but Hayley's soothing touch had stirred him in places he hadn't visited in years.

He gave himself a mental shake and, dragging himself to his feet, staggered back out to his bed.

* * *

'He's in the bathroom,' Hayley said, leading Dr Alistair Preece into the bedroom, but when she saw the figure splayed out on the bed she quickly amended, 'Oh, I mean he's in here.'

She stood to one side as the doctor asked Jasper a series of questions, including what he'd eaten in the last forty-eight hours. He also took his blood pressure and some blood to send off for testing, but his diagnosis leaned towards a rather nasty stomach virus that was currently doing the rounds.

'It should pass in a day or so,' Dr Preece addressed Hayley. 'I suggest he stays in bed, push the fluids as tolerated, especially those electrolyte replacement drinks you can get from a pharmacy, but if things don't improve take him to your nearest outpatients' department for admission for IV rehydration.'

Hayley saw the doctor out and came back to find Jasper heading back to the *en suite*. 'Are you going to be sick again?'

'No,' he said. 'I thought I'd have a shower.'

She made sure he had enough towels and closed the door and went back to strip the bed so she could put on fresh sheets. It took her a few minutes to find them in the linen cupboard further along the hall, but the task was soon completed.

Jasper came back out of the *en suite* and saw the freshly made bed. 'You didn't have to do that,' he said, frowning slightly.

'It was no trouble.' She peeled back the top sheet and turned her back as he dropped his towel. She waited until she was sure he was covered before she turned back round. 'I'm going to duck out to get some of that fluid-replacement stuff the doctor recommended. That's probably why your headache is so bad. It's caused by dehydration. Will you be OK while I'm gone?'

He nodded even though it sent a tremor worthy of the upper end of the Richter scale through his head. 'Eric left your car keys on the hall table downstairs,' he said. 'But you can take mine if you like.'

'No, I prefer my own. Just close your eyes and I'll be back as soon as I can.'

Jasper opened his eyes a short time later to see her standing by his bedside with a vile coloured drink in her hands.

'You need to do this slowly,' she said, propping the glass up to his mouth. 'Just take a few sips to see if they stay down.'

He found it hard to concentrate when the shadow of her cleavage was the only thing he could see. He forced his eyes closed and took a sip, his tight throat relaxing as the liquid went down. 'I wonder if this is an omen or something,' he said, laying his head back on the soft mound of pillows she had arranged. 'Maybe Raymond's put a curse on me for marrying you for all the wrong reasons.'

'He came to see me while you were away.'

He cranked his eyes open to look at her. 'Oh, really? What did he do? Try to warn you off?'

'Sort of.'

He closed his eyes again. 'It obviously didn't work, then.'

'You didn't really leave me much choice,' she pointed out. 'I had to marry you to save my business.'

'I had to marry you to save my inheritance,' he returned. 'There was no other way.'

'I never thought my life would be like this,' she said after a moment's silence. 'I somehow thought my wedding day would be…you know…different from this.'

'I guess the groom lying on the bathroom floor isn't a part of any young girl's dream of her special day,' he commented dryly.

A reluctant wry smile spread across her face. 'No, it isn't,' she said. 'I had visions of champagne bubbling in tall crystal glasses and rose petals strewn across the bed and soft music playing.'

'So I took a creative detour,' he said. 'Try not to hold it against me. I might just make it up to you in the end.'

'Somehow I don't think so.'

'Because you really wanted Myles?' he asked, looking at her again.

Hayley had trouble for a moment even recalling what her ex-fiancé looked like. 'I wanted to marry a man who loved me,' she said, looking at her hands rather than into his dark, contemplative gaze. 'Is that so much for a girl to ask?'

'Your head is full of romantic dreams that rarely come true in real life,' he said. 'Most couples fall out of love before the second anniversary.'

She raised her eyes back to his. 'But true love does happen occasionally, look at the Hendersons.'

'Perhaps now and again a couple might find a certain chemistry that lasts the distance, but it's still extremely rare,' he acceded.

The silence was so acute Hayley heard the soft sound of the sheets rustling when one of his feet moved in the bed next to her thigh.

'You're still young, Hayley,' he said. 'You'll find someone else as soon as we divorce, someone much better than Myles, and certainly a whole lot better than me.'

'It's not easy meeting nice men these days,' she said. 'I thought I got it right with Myles but now I'm not so sure. How can I trust my judgement any more?'

'So you're finally prepared to admit you're not in love with him?'

Her eyes came back to his. 'He was the very first man to tell me he loved me. I guess I got swept up with the notion of belonging to someone.'

A small frown appeared between his brows. 'Didn't my father ever tell you how much he loved you?'

She shook her head. 'Not in so many words, but I always knew he did. I guess he just wasn't comfortable expressing it out loud.'

Jasper laid his head back on the pillows and closed his eyes. 'You deserved better than this, Hayley. I still can't quite figure out why the old guy left things so complicated. I know he was determined to pull me in line, but I don't see why he had to use you to do it.'

'It's OK, Jasper,' she said, touching his hand where it lay on the bed. 'It's not for long and then you will have what you want.'

He opened his eyes to meet hers, his expression hard to decode. 'But what about what you want?' he asked, his hand turning over to entrap her fingers.

Her breath locked in her throat as the warmth of his hand seeped into hers. 'I guess what I want can wait a little longer,' she said.

He gave her fingers a tiny squeeze and closed his eyes once more. 'This is day one, only thirty more to go.'

Hayley looked at their loosely linked hands and suppressed an inner sigh. He was already counting the days until he would be free while she was treasuring each moment they were together, storing away the memories of each time he touched her to see her through the long lonely days ahead.

She longed to feel his mouth on hers again; the shifting moods of his lips and tongue fascinated her. He could kiss with such softness and yet with such hard determination, each stroke and glide of his tongue making her boneless and weak with desire. The press of his body against hers was now printed indelibly on her memory. Even looking at him lying supine on the bed beside her she could almost feel his hard, muscular chest against the softness of her breasts, and her nipples began to tighten with longing beneath the light fabric of her night-gown and wrap. Her eyes travelled lower to where the sheet covered his hips and pelvis, and her stomach hollowed as she recalled how he had felt fully aroused. It didn't take too much imagination on her part to imagine how exciting and fulfilling making love with him would be. His mouth tasted of sex every time he kissed her, the heat and fire of his touch leaving her in no doubt of his sensual expertise.

She lifted her free hand to his brow once more, her touch soft as a feather in case she disturbed his slumber. He was still warm but not beaded with perspiration as he had been earlier.

She traced each of his dark brows with one of her fingertips, then over the mauve satin of each of his eyelids, marvelling at the length of his sooty lashes, which lay like twin fans against his cheeks. She travelled down the length of his nose before hovering near the temptation of his mouth for a moment or two.

She drew in a tiny breath that caught at her throat as she began to gently outline his upper lip, a tiny shiver passing over her skin as the soft pad of her fingertip encountered the sexy rasp of his evening stubble. Her finger moved to his bottom lip, lingering over its sensual fullness, her mouth tingling as she thought of how it had felt to have those lips burning against hers.

Almost without realising she was doing it, she leaned forward and pressed a whisper of a kiss against his lips, the tip of her tongue sneaking out to anoint his dryness with her moistness. She heard him groan softly and pulled back from him, her heart suddenly racing. But after a few more minutes sitting watching him she realised he was soundly asleep and her heart rate gradually returned to normal.

She stifled a yawn and settled down beside him, promising herself she'd wake before he did and go back to her room…

CHAPTER TEN

HAYLEY OPENED HER eyes just as dawn broke to see Jasper propped up on one elbow, his dark gaze trained on her.

'How are you feeling?' she asked, her voice coming out like the sound of a creaky door opening.

'I'm feeling fine,' he said. 'How about you?'

She blinked at him a little vacantly. 'Me?'

He brushed some of her wayward curls off her face. 'Yes, you. I haven't infected you, have I?'

She felt her spine loosen as his fingers secured her hair behind her ear. 'Not so far.'

His eyes held hers in a silence that began to hum with erotic promise. Hayley was suddenly all too conscious of how close her bare legs were to his—her nightgown had somehow worked its way up around her waist and her wrap was on the floor where she must have discarded it during the night.

He placed a gentle hand to her forehead. 'You feel a bit hot,' he said.

'It's only because I've been sleeping with you... I mean, not exactly *sleeping* with you, but...well...you know what I mean...'

He picked up another strand of her hair, but instead of securing it behind her ear he coiled it around his finger, his eyes still locked with hers. 'I had this really weird dream last night,' he said.

'Oh?' She moistened her mouth with the tip of her tongue. 'W-what was it about?'

His eyes left hers briefly to look down at her mouth, lingering there for a moment before returning to her blue-green gaze. 'I dreamt that I made passionate love to you.'

She tried to affect a flippant tone. 'Wow, that is weird.'

'But what's even weirder is finding you in my bed this morning.' He released her hair as a small frown brought his brows closer. 'I didn't do anything to you that you didn't want me to, did I?'

Hayley was both surprised and touched by the obvious concern in his tone. She hadn't thought him capable of a conscience, especially when it came to having his own way. 'No, of course you didn't.'

His frown still hovered on his forehead. 'Did we make love?'

Hayley could feel her cheeks firing. 'No.'

'So nothing happened?'

'Nothing happened, Jasper.'

Silence.

Heavy beating silence.

'I had this other dream,' he said, his gaze going to her mouth once more. 'Or at least I think it was a dream but I could be wrong. It might very well have happened for real.'

The brush of his gaze made Hayley's lips tingle but somehow she managed to croak out, 'Oh?'

'I dreamt that you kissed me.'

She shifted her eyes from the laser beam intensity of his. 'You were probably dreaming of the kiss at the wedding...'

'I don't think so.' He brought her chin up and looked deep into her eyes. 'Why did you kiss me, Hayley?'

'I was tired and not thinking straight. I'm sorry. It won't happen again.'

'You don't need to apologise and I want it to happen again. I've been thinking about it while I watched you sleeping, imagining what it would feel like to be inside you. My body's been on fire for the past hour.'

'Jasper, I…' She stopped to run her tongue over her dry lips again, her stomach feeling as if a giant hole had just opened in it as he leaned closer.

'Tell me you don't want to make love with me,' he said, pressing a kiss to the side of her neck. 'Tell me and I'll stop right now.'

How could she even think straight, let alone speak with his tongue rasping along the sensitive skin stretched over her collar-bone? Hayley wondered. How could she deny herself the feel of his weight pinning her to the bed, and the plunge of his hard body into the needy softness of hers?

He kissed the side of her mouth, his tongue flicking against her bottom lip, once, twice, three times. 'Do you want me to stop?' he asked, his voice so deep she felt it rumble against her breasts.

'No…' she said, and, stifling a groan, brought her mouth to his in a hot, slippery kiss that said more than words ever could. Her hands went to his hair, her fingers burying in its thickness to keep him tethered to her mouth. His tongue set fire to her mouth, each possessive thrust thrilling her as she felt the heat and probe of his erection between her legs as he rolled with her so she was on her back. She felt the abrasion of his leg hair against her silky smoothness and opened her thighs to accommodate him further, her indrawn breath scalding her throat as she felt him brush up against her tender folds, the barely leashed power of his body totally thrilling her.

His mouth moved from its passionate onslaught on hers to suckle on her right breast through the silk of her nightgown, which to Hayley seemed all the more erotic than if he had removed the fabric from her body. She looked down at his dark head and felt a shock wave of delight pass through her belly as his mouth drew hard on her nipple, carrying an electric charge right through her body. He moved to her other breast and did the same, and then, just when she thought she could stand it no longer, he pushed the straps of her nightgown down past her shoulders and uncovered her breasts. She felt the scorch of his gaze as he looked down at her creamy shape, the rose-tipped nipples proudly erect.

'You are so perfect,' he said, shaping her with his hand, his eyes burning with arousal. 'So very beautiful.'

She sucked in a breath as he bent his head to each nipple, his tongue rolling over and over each tight point until she was writhing beneath him.

One of his hands moved between their bodies and searched for her heated warmth, his fingers opening her gently as he felt the silky moistness. She gasped with pleasure as he stroked the swollen heart of her with expert precision, her nerves quivering in escalating excitement as the pressure for release built, making her feel as if her body were hovering on the edge of a very steep precipice.

'You feel so ready for me,' he groaned against her mouth. 'So tight and wet.'

She was beyond speech; all she could do was feel what he was doing to her. Her whole body was zinging with spiralling sensations as his mouth left hers to kiss a blazing pathway down her body, dawdling over her breasts, stopping at her belly button just long enough to set it alight, before he went to where every nerve in her body seemed to have gathered in one tiny pearl of pressure that ached and pulsed to be released.

The first hot flicker of his tongue arched her back, her whimpering cry rising high in the air as he did it again and again. She couldn't hold back the storm of sensation that exploded in her body like a volcano that had waited years to erupt. She felt each earth-shattering tremor and the delicious aftershocks in every part of her body, leaving her weak and spent in his arms.

He reached for a condom in the bedside chest of drawers and she watched with bated breath, her excitement building all over again as she saw him apply it to his length.

He came back over her, his mouth taking hers in a hard, probing kiss as his body surged forward into her honeyed warmth. Hayley flinched as he entered her, her inner muscles untrained at accepting the unfamiliar length and breadth of him.

Jasper stilled his movements and, holding himself up on his bent arms, looked at her in concern. 'Am I rushing you?'

'No…no, of course not,' she said, pressing her spine into the mattress in an effort to relax.

A small frown appeared on his forehead. 'You *have* had sex before, haven't you?'

'Of course I have.'

'How many times?'

'Um…just the once…'

He let out an expletive and began to withdraw.

'No!' She clutched at him to keep him inside her. 'I want this to be special. My first time was a disaster…that's why I never really got around to repeating it.'

His frown became even heavier. 'Did he force himself on you?'

'No, of course not,' she said. 'We were both young and in-experienced. He didn't know what he was doing and I certainly wasn't much help. It was over before it began.'

'I wish you had told me,' he said, still frowning. 'I could have taken things a little slower. Did I hurt you?'

'Not really…'

He tipped up her chin and made her lock gazes with him. 'Did I hurt you, Hayley?'

She compressed her lips, the sudden urge to cry taking her completely by surprise. 'Not much…' she whispered.

He swore again and began to pull out, but she anticipated it and grasped at his buttocks, digging her fingers in. 'Please show me what the fuss is all about,' she said. 'Please, Jasper. I want to know how it feels to come during sex. I've never felt that before. For years I've felt like a failure in bed. Make me feel like a woman should feel.'

He hesitated, but Hayley could already feel his body stirring within the tight sheath of hers. She tensed and released her inner muscles and he groaned and sank forward, his control slipping. She felt every thrust, the first ones restrained, cautious and tender until his control finally slipped out of his reach. He began to increase his pace, his breathing rate rising, the tension in his body building as he drove on, each surging movement bringing her closer to the point of no return. It was beyond anything she could have imagined to feel his strength and heat and passion filling her so completely. The musky scent of him, the salty taste of his skin, the rough abrasion of his masculine jaw on the tender softness of her face were so incredibly sensual and exciting.

His mouth became increasingly demanding and his tongue commanding in its subjugation of hers. She returned his fiery kiss with growing urgency, her tongue flicking against his, her hands stroking the sweat-slicked skin of his back as he rocked with escalating need against her. Her body tightened around him, holding him, releasing him, holding him until she heard him suck in a tight breath as he desperately fought for control.

He caressed her intimately, coaxing her back to paradise with ever quickening strokes that sent her beyond thought as her body prepared itself for another free fall of rapture. Every nerve tightened, every sensory outlet jangling with need until she was perched on the edge again, her body straining for the final lift off. As if he sensed she was ready to fly again, she felt his whole body tensing momentarily, before he surged forward again with a series of pumping explosive thrusts that triggered her release, his breath whooshing out on a deep groan of satisfaction in the afterglow of his own.

Hayley's body felt as if it had been shattered into a thousand tiny pieces and now each one of them was floating back down to the bed to resume its place on her person. Her breathing was still out of order, her belly still quivering with the tremors that had rocked her to the core.

She watched as Jasper rolled away, his strong, muscular body delighting her all over again. She reached out a hand and stroked it down the length of his flank, her eyes meeting his as he turned back to face her.

'Still want to play, baby girl?' he asked with a dangerously sexy smile lighting his brown-black gaze.

Hayley was surprised at her own boldness; she had never felt so sensually alive and confident before. She stroked her fingers upwards from his thigh, bending forward to press her mouth against the jut of his hip, her tongue doing little circles, wider and wider until he was flat on his back, his growing arousal so close to her mouth she saw his chest and abdomen pull in sharply in anticipation. It was an intoxicating sense of power to have him lying under her command, his whole body quivering as she came closer and closer with her lips in hot, moist little kisses.

She heard him muffle a rough expletive as her lips brushed against him tentatively, the ridged muscles of his abdomen tensing as she moistened her mouth with her tongue. His hands clenched the sheets either side of his body as she tasted him, a groan coming from deep inside him as she stroked her tongue over him experimentally.

'Where the hell did you learn to do that?' he asked on the tail end of another ragged groan.

Hayley smiled a secret smile and bent her head to take him fully in her mouth, her stomach kicking in excitement when she felt his jerk of surprise and delight as her tongue moved in circular movements over him. She drew on him boldly, the sensation of his power and strength against the softness of her mouth totally enthralling.

'Oh, God, I can't hold back…' Jasper gasped and tried to pull away but she splayed her palm on the flat, hard plane of his belly and kept him where she wanted him.

It was the most erotic experience of his life to have her receive him in such an intimate way. He shuddered his way through it, his whole body shivering with the mind-blowing pleasure of her mouth.

He lay back with his eyes tightly closed, trying to get his breathing under control, wondering when he had ever felt this totally perfect physical connection with another lover. It was almost visceral the way her body responded to his and his to hers. He had never experienced anything like it before, the fine-tuning of their bodies producing such harmonious accord he felt as if every other sexual encounter he'd experienced in the past had somehow robbed him short.

He opened his eyes to see her looking at him, a tentative, almost shy smile playing at her mouth. He reached out his hand and brought her silky head to his chest, the feel of her cloud of dark hair against his naked skin making something constrict almost painfully deep inside him.

'No one's ever done that before,' he said into the silence.

'What?' The movement of air from her mouth as she spoke danced over the indentation of his belly button.

'Without a condom, I mean,' he said, lacing his fingers through her hair. 'It's totally different; amazing, in fact.'

Hayley stroked his thigh with her fingertip, her cheek so close to his heart she could feel it beating, and the pulse of his body ricocheting through hers. She ran her fingers up and down his thigh for a moment before turning away to get off the bed.

'Where are you going?' Jasper asked.

'I'm going to have a shower,' she said, scooping up her wrap from the floor and covering her nakedness with a modesty he found rather ironic. 'If we're going to make that flight in time we should get a move on.'

'You still want to go?'

'Do you feel up to it?' she asked.

'I'm surprised you even felt the need to ask that,' he said, throwing his legs over the edge of the bed and getting to his feet. 'I thought I had rather convincingly assured you that, in spite of last night's aberration I was once again in the best of health.'

Her gaze fell away from his. 'I was so worried about you.'

He closed the distance between them with two strides and lifted her chin. 'I must say I like the way you show your concern,' he said with a wry smile.

'It was just sex, Jasper,' she said crushingly, more to remind herself of their arrangement than anything. 'Nothing more.'

His hand dropped from her face. 'Is that all you want from me? Just sex?'

Her blue-green eyes were steady as they held his gaze. 'That's all you have to offer, isn't it, Jasper? Just sex. No commitment, no long term future—just sex.'

'Are you going to be happy with that?'

Hayley had to fight to control her expression so she didn't give away her longing for more than he could offer. 'This thing that's happening between us will burn out over time. It might not even last the month.'

'You think so?'

She gave him a world-weary smile. 'I *know* so, Jasper. You haven't had a relationship last longer than a month or two. I'm not your type, for one thing, and then there's the issue of our separation in a month's time. I want kids and a house in the suburbs. You want a playboy lifestyle with no attachments.'

'But we could do this for now,' Jasper ventured, gauging her reaction closely. 'Just for the time being, to see how it goes. What do you think?'

'We could,' she said, her expression for once giving him no clue. 'But wouldn't that be asking for complications when the clock runs out?'

'We could extend the time,' he suggested. 'We don't have to separate right on the dot at the end of the month.'

'For what purpose? I want totally different things from life. You'd only be holding me up from what I want in order to continue a relationship that in the end is really going nowhere.'

'I want you, Hayley,' he said as she turned for the bathroom. 'And you want me.'

She turned back to look at him. 'But for how long?'

'That's a hard question to answer. A week, a month, two months. Who knows?'

'But not for ever,' she said with a soft little sigh. 'You're not a for ever guy.'

'No one can promise for ever,' he said heavily. 'Life is not predictable. Anything can happen; you of all people should know that.'

'I *do* know that,' she answered. 'But that's why I want stability in my life now. I crave it.'

'I can't promise to give you what you want in the long term, but I can do here and now.'

'Here and now sounds like a consolation prize,' she said.

'Maybe it is,' he said. 'But it's better than being left empty-handed, isn't it?'

Being left empty-hearted is the thing I'm most concerned about, Hayley thought as she turned on the shower a few moments later. It seemed both her future and her happiness were now in the hands of Jasper Caulfield, the man who had already left one woman in the lurch. Would she be yet another casualty?

CHAPTER ELEVEN

HAYLEY LOOKED AT the travel itinerary with a frown when they arrived at the airport. 'I think someone's made a mistake,' she said, looking up at Jasper. 'This says we're going to Bedarra Island, but Myles and I were supposed to be going to Green Island for our honeymoon.'

Jasper put their luggage on the conveyor belt before turning back to face her. 'I took the liberty of changing your booking. I didn't want you moping about missing him. Bedarra is much more private and exclusive.'

She stood back as their boarding passes were issued, her frown deepening as she thought about the renowned romantic getaway that contained only sixteen private freestanding villas, each one built around the beautiful natural tropical rainforest landscape with spectacular ocean views over neighbouring islands on the Capricorn coast. It was the destination for honeymooners with money to spare and the desire to be totally alone.

A short time later they boarded the flight to Cairns, and Hayley immediately buried her head in a book, but every now and again her gaze slid sideways to where Jasper appeared to be dozing by her side, his face still lacking the colour she was used to seeing there in spite of his assurances he was feeling fine.

The forty-minute connecting flight from Cairns to Dunk Island where they were to meet the launch for the fifteen-minute transfer to Bedarra Island seemed to strip his face of even more colour.

'Are you feeling OK?' she asked, touching his hand where it gripped the arm-rest rather tightly as they came in to land.

'Yep,' he said, rubbing at his face as he straightened in his seat. 'How about you?'

'I'm fine.'

'Not sore?'

She looked away from the concern she could see in his dark eyes, her cheeks feeling hot all of a sudden. 'No.'

He gave her hand a tiny squeeze. 'You wouldn't tell me if you were, now, would you?'

She brought her gaze back to his, her expression rueful. 'No, probably not.'

He lifted her hand to his mouth, pressing a soft kiss to her fingertips, his eyes holding hers. 'I will be gentle with you, baby girl,' he said. 'It takes time to get used to a new lover.'

Hayley was glad of the distraction of landing and then transferring from the flight to the boat that took them to Bedarra Island. Her body was still acutely aware of how Jasper had possessed her. Every time she took a step she felt a fluttery sensation between her thighs as if he were still there, pulsing with heat and passion.

The sun was dappling the water as they were led to their villa, the sweet and moist fragrance of the tropics filling her nostrils as they walked past beautifully landscaped gardens.

Once their attendant had left Jasper lifted the bottle of Bollinger out of the ice bucket and began to pour some into the two glasses. 'So what do you think?' he asked, handing her a glass fizzing with exquisite bubbles.

Hayley cradled her drink and looked around the luxurious

premium split-level villa with amazement. It offered the ultimate in privacy and overlooked the sparkling ocean, the private balcony complete with spa.

'It's fabulous,' she said, taking a tentative sip of the delicious champagne. 'But you really didn't need to change the booking. It must have cost you an arm and a leg.'

'What if it did?' he said. 'Since I don't intend to go on another honeymoon in this lifetime I thought I should do this one properly.'

Hayley felt a crushing disappointment in the middle of her chest. It had never been his intention to marry anyone, least of all her, but did he have to keep reminding her of it?

He raised his glass to hers. 'So let's drink to being together for a month.'

Hayley chinked her glass against his. 'To a month of madness,' she said.

His mouth twisted as he returned the toast. 'Is that what you think it will be?'

'What else can it be?' she asked. 'The last person in the world you want to be married to is me, even short term.'

Jasper frowned at the hint of despondency in her tone. 'Listen, sweetheart,' he said. 'Don't go taking it personally. Marriage has never been my thing. I told you that.'

She looked up at him with eyes the colour of the ocean outside. 'Don't you want more out of life, Jasper?' she asked in a breathy whisper. 'You know…someone to come home to each day, someone to talk to about your life, the ups and downs, sharing in the intimacy of companionship.'

He put his drink down with a hard little crack on the nearest surface. 'Stop it, Hayley,' he said. 'Stop this nonsense right now. You know the deal. This is not permanent.'

'You can't live the rest of your life alone,' she said. 'Everyone needs someone some time.'

'You sound like the lyrics to a song,' he said with a lip curl of derision. 'Get rid of your romantic dreams. I'm not your guy.'

She bit her lip as she stared down at the dancing bubbles in her glass. 'No I know,' she said. 'But it's nice to hear the words *"I love you"*.'

His forehead became a map of frowning lines. 'I knew sleeping with you would be a mistake,' he growled. 'You just don't get it, do you? It's not your fault, you're a sweet kid and all that, but I can't offer you more than this brief period of time.'

Tears of hurt shone in her eyes. 'You used my weakness where you're concerned to get what you want,' she said. 'I can see it now. You knew I wouldn't marry you unless you bribed me into it and, just to make sure in case the bribes didn't work, you set about to make me fall hopelessly head over heels for you.'

He stared at her. 'Is that what you think I set out to do?'

Her bottom lip trembled. 'Isn't it?'

He raised his eyes heavenwards. 'I hope you're happy now, you sick old bastard,' he muttered under his breath before he returned his gaze to Hayley's. 'No, it isn't. You're getting physical attraction confused with other emotions.'

'So you at least admit you're attracted to me?'

He gave her an ironic look. 'I can hardly contest that when on a couple of occasions you've held the evidence in your hands or mouth, not to mention your body, now can I?'

'You used me to get what you want. You saw my vulnerability and went for it like a jungle cat goes for the jugular.'

There was a small pulsing silence.

'Are you telling me you're in love with me?' he asked.

Hayley couldn't hold his piercing gaze. 'No, of course not,' she said. 'I'm not *that* stupid.'

'But you *are* attracted to me.'

'I'm sure it won't last very long,' she said, scraping her pride together with an effort. 'I'm ashamed of myself for responding to you.'

'Is this about Myles again? He betrayed you. He was a player, Hayley. He was getting his rocks off with whoever was available.'

She sent him a caustic glare. 'No doubt it takes one to know one,' she bit out. 'You're hardly one to criticise the sexual exploits of another man when you've set the playboy benchmark.'

'At least I'm honest about my intentions. I don't believe in making promises I know I won't be able to keep. I told you the score from the word go. I can't help it if you chose to ignore my warnings and get your heart broken in the process. '

She looked at him through eyes glittering with angry tears. 'You're an unfeeling bastard,' she said. 'You don't care about another person but yourself, do you? Everything you do in life is for you. It has been for years. If I was Daniel Moorebank I would be ashamed to call you my father. You're not worthy of the title.'

Fury suddenly flashed in his dark gaze as it hit hers. 'You don't know what you're talking about, you spiteful little cat. You know nothing of the situation.'

She sent him a venomous glare. 'From what I've heard from Miriam's new husband, you've consistently refused to support Daniel. How can you turn your back on your own son like that?'

'So you've met Martin Beckforth, have you?' he asked with a derisory twist to his mouth.

She glowered at him. 'He came in to pick his mum up a couple of months ago when her car was in the workshop. It's not easy being a stepfather and the job is even harder if the real father is not paying his way.'

His mouth was set in a white line of anger. 'I don't mind supporting Daniel, but I refuse to support that layabout jerk.'

'He's nothing of the sort,' she threw back. 'He seemed very nice and extremely concerned about Daniel, who is turning out to be a handful.'

'Stay out of my life, Hayley,' he said through clenched teeth. 'You can sleep in my bed any time you like, but stay the hell out of my personal life.'

Hayley watched as he swung away to leave the villa, the door snapping shut behind him rattling the glasses on the silver tray.

She didn't see him for the rest of the evening, which made her anger towards him move upwards another notch. She felt stupid sitting in the open terrace restaurant by herself, picking at the delicious food and sipping at the wine the attentive waiter provided while the other couples sat there in romantic, companionable bliss.

Finally she gave up and went for a walk along the beach, taking off her sandals so she could bury her toes in the powdery sand. The moon was a silver sickle in the sky and a few stars were peeping through the blue-black velvet blanket of the sky.

She saw a lone figure standing at one end of the strip of sand, his tall, athletic frame silhouetted by the lights shining from the terrace. He was throwing tiny pebbles into the water, one after one, skimming them along the surface, the dancing movements making popping noises in the stillness of the tropical night air.

She had seen him do the very same thing down at the Crickglades pond in the past. Even way back then she had been able to discern his moods by the force of each throw; the size of the missile had warned her on many an occasion to stay well away.

She suspected that if a decent sized rock were available now he would be using that to vent his anger. His every movement seemed to suggest he was coiled with tension, his back was rigid with it, and as she moved closer she could see the hardened line of his jaw as he aimed another throw.

He must have sensed her presence for he turned and looked at her, his eyes running over her like a hot flame. 'If you're after an apology I'm not giving it to you,' he said, bending down to search for another pebble. He straightened and threw it as far as he could, the sound of it hitting the water fracturing the silence.

'I felt like an idiot up there eating by myself,' she bit out resentfully. 'The least you could have done is brush off your surly attitude and play the role of attentive husband. That's the deal, remember? When we're in public we're supposed to be acting as if everything is normal between us.'

He stepped towards her, standing so close she felt her neck crick to keep eye contact. 'What's wrong, baby girl? Feeling lonely all of a sudden?'

'You're horrid.'

'And you are a nosy little bitch.'

She clenched her fists at her sides, determined not to slap him even though she dearly longed to. 'I wish I had never agreed to this charade.'

'Then why did you?' he asked.

'You know why.'

His smile bordered on a smirk. 'Because you couldn't resist me? Go on, admit it, Hayley. You wanted to do it with me, didn't you? You've wanted to for years.'

'I'm going to make you regret this, you know,' she warned him recklessly. 'You will seriously regret marrying me, I guarantee it.'

His eyes glittered as he took her upper arms in his hands,

his fingers biting almost cruelly. 'You are just like every other woman I know—greedy and grasping. But I should warn you, sweetheart, that I won't let you get away with it. If you want to thrash it out once our marriage is over I'm well prepared for it. I have some cards up my sleeve that will make you think twice about playing hardball with me.'

Her eyes flashed at him in the moonlight. 'I hate you.'

'That's more like it,' he drawled as he dropped his hands. 'I was starting to worry you were forming a bit of an attachment to me.'

She rolled her eyes. 'As if I would be that stupid.'

'Don't confuse good old fashioned lust with love, Hayley,' he said. 'We can get down and dirty whenever you want, but don't go wrapping it up in anything other than what it is.'

'I. Hate. You. I can't bear the thought of you touching me.'

'Liar.'

'I mean it.' She lifted her chin.

He gave a mocking laugh. 'You are so pathetic at lying. Ever since you were sixteen years old you've been begging me to give you a good—'

She raised her hand and slapped him before he could say the crude word, the sound of her palm connecting with his cheek ringing in the still night air, her hand instantly burning from the contact.

The throbbing silence was menacing. It swirled around them amongst the shadows, creeping closer and closer until Hayley was sure she was going to be swallowed whole by it.

'You know,' he said in a tone that contained an unmistakable steely edge, 'you really shouldn't have done that.'

She fought hard against the trepidation that was filling her throat, making it difficult for her to swallow. 'You asked for it,' she said.

'I could say the same about you,' he returned, taking a

handful of her hair, his fingers lifting the skin of her scalp as he brought her one step closer to his hard body. 'You're still begging for it, aren't you, Hayley? You've been begging for it for years. You want me to throw you down on the sand at our feet and show you just how ruthless I can be. Go on, admit it.'

He gave a taunting laugh and tapped her on the end of her nose as he said each word. 'You. Want. Me. Want me to prove it?'

She gritted her teeth. 'Get your filthy hands off me.'

He pulled her even closer, his mouth now hardly a breath away from hers. 'Make me,' he said, his eyes narrowed and glinting in sexy temptation. 'Go on. I dare you.'

Hayley was beyond thought or reason. Her body felt as if it were being fuelled by a bewildering combination of anger to push him away, and an even greater desire to pull him closer and have him do what he had suggested. She felt her toes curl into the sand beneath her feet, his body so close she could feel the pulse of his erection as it pressed against her quivering belly. His mouth met hers, or maybe hers met his—she wasn't entirely sure who had made that last devastating movement, but when it happened it was like an earthquake rumbling through her whole being.

His tongue met hers somewhere in the middle, curling around hers, fighting with it, subduing it and then seducing it until she felt her legs go from beneath her. The soft sand cushioned her back as he came down with her, his body weight crushing her beneath him, his long, strong legs entrapping hers.

His hands tugged the shoestring straps of her dress down so he could access her breasts with the heat of his palms, the rough stroke of his thumbs over her nipples making them instantly peak in pleasure. His mouth came down over her right nipple, his tongue playing with it before he suckled on her, his teeth nipping at her tantalisingly before he moved to her other breast. It was wild and abandoned; the hot brand of his mouth, the rasp of his tongue and the sensual scrape of his teeth as he toyed with her, each of his caresses making her senses spin out of control.

She tore at his open cotton shirt, dragging it from his shoulders, her mouth pressed hotly to the side of his neck where she could feel his pulse thumping. She sucked on his salty skin before using her teeth to bite him, neither hard nor gently but somewhere in between, her tongue rolling over the imprint of the mark she'd made.

In amongst his ragged breathing she heard him groan as his hand pulled up her dress, tugging her tiny lacy knickers to one side so he could find the pulsing heart of her. She felt the plunge of his fingers inside her wet warmth and whimpered in delight, her pelvis lifting to bring him deeper. She tugged at the waistband of his shorts, pulling them down, his aroused body jutting towards her scented core like an arrow to a target.

She gasped in pleasure at the first deep thrust, her fingers digging into his taut buttocks to anchor herself as he drove again and again, each time harder and deeper until she was panting to keep up to his frantic rhythm. His body rocked against hers, his chest slick with sweat as he brought her closer and closer to the point of earth-shattering rapture. She could feel it building in every nerve in her body, her back arching, her legs tensing as with one last mind-blowing thrust he tipped her over the edge into the cascading, thunderous waterfall of her release.

She felt his pumping action inside her as she floated in the shallows of satisfaction, the burst of his life force dragging a deep guttural groan from the depths of his chest as he finally let go. She felt the aftershocks through the skin of his back, his muscles twitching as her fingers drifted over him.

But she felt herself instantly shrink in shame as soon as he lifted himself off her, his expression brooding as he reached for his shorts and shirt. 'You'd better cover yourself,' he said. 'I can hear someone coming.'

She scrambled to her feet, pulling her straps back over her shoulders, the rest of her dress falling into place around her knees as she turned and stumbled to the path that led back to their villa.

Jasper waited until she'd disappeared around the curve of the path before he bent down to the sand and picked up her sandals. He dangled them from one hand for a moment, and then at a much slower pace followed in the direction she went, a heavy frown settling between his brows.

CHAPTER TWELVE

HAYLEY CAME OUT of the shower a long time later, pointedly avoiding Jasper's eyes as she came into the main bedroom suite.

'Hayley, we need to talk.'

She turned her back and rummaged through her open suitcase for her nightwear. 'I'd rather not, if you don't mind,' she clipped out.

She heard him let out a frustrated sigh before she felt his hand on her arm turning her around to face him.

'Listen to me, Hayley,' he began.

She slapped at his hand as if it were a mosquito. 'I don't want to talk to you. I don't want anything to do with you. You're an arrogant pig, that's what you are.'

His hold tightened. 'Will you shut up and listen to me, for God's sake?' he growled.

She fought against the tremble of her bottom lip. 'You took advantage of me,' she accused.

His expression hardened. 'I did not do any such thing. You could have stopped me at any point but you didn't. You were with me all the way.'

Her eyes flashed with blue and green sparks of anger. 'You make it impossible to resist you, that's why! I hate you for that!'

'It's hardly my fault if you have no self-control.'

'You're the one with no self-control,' she threw back. 'You didn't even use protection.'

His eyes bored into hers. 'That's what I want to talk to you about. Are you on the contraceptive pill?'

'I don't have to tell you my personal details,' she said. 'We're only going to be together a month. I don't have to even tell you my shoe size if I don't want to.'

'I already know your shoe size. You left your sandals on the beach.'

'I also left my dignity on the beach,' she tossed back. 'Did you happen to pick that up as well?'

It was a full thirty seconds before he spoke, each and every one of them seeming endless as he stood looking down at her with those dark, unfathomable eyes.

'I'm sorry,' he said at last, his voice sounding rough and uneven. 'I probably hurt you.'

Hayley felt her defences ambushed by his change of tone. Her anger melted and she suddenly felt close to tears. 'It's all right,' she mumbled, looking away. 'I shouldn't have slapped you. I detest violence of any sort. I'm deeply ashamed of myself.'

He captured her chin and brought her gaze back to his. 'No, you shouldn't have slapped me, but then I probably goaded you into it. We do seem to have the strangest effect on each other, don't we? One minute I want to shake you until your teeth rattle and the next I want to bury myself inside you and explode.'

Hayley felt the sharp tug of desire in her lower body at his gruff confession. 'I feel like that too,' she whispered.

'But therein lies our current problem,' he said. 'As you say, I didn't use protection, which raises a rather important issue.'

'I'm in a safe time…' *I think,* she mentally crossed her fingers.

'Our situation would become rather complicated if you were to fall pregnant,' he said.

'I have no intention of falling pregnant.'

'Are you saying that from the standpoint of pharmaceutical back up or from a totally irrational feminine hunch?'

She forced herself to meet his probing gaze. 'I'm saying there's no chance I could fall pregnant right now.'

'You seem very sure.'

'I know my own body.'

'I won't allow it to happen again,' he said.

Her face fell before she could stop it. 'You mean you're not going to…I mean…we're not going to…' Her cheeks flamed with colour at his amused look as she faltered.

'Have sex?'

'Um…yes…'

'I thought you couldn't stand the thought of me touching you?' he said. 'Am I to take it you've changed your mind?'

Hayley looked into the depths of dark, tempting gaze and inwardly sighed. How could she tell him she wanted him to feel for her how she felt for him? She couldn't, but she also knew there was no way she could offer any other answer than the one her body had already given him.

'It's only for a month,' she said, pleased that her voice sounded so relaxed and casual about it all. 'Why don't we enjoy this while it lasts?'

'Are you sure about that?'

She gave him a bright smile even though inside she could feel her heart contracting painfully. 'I'm a modern girl,' she assured him. 'Having a sex buddy is all the rage at the moment. Lucky me to have such an experienced one.'

A small frown pulled at his brow. 'So you're happy with no-strings sex?'

'Of course. Why shouldn't I be? After all, that's what you want, isn't it?' she asked.

'I don't want you to get the wrong idea about any of this,'

he said, still frowning as he released her. 'I wouldn't want you to get your hopes up for a happy ever after with me because it's just not going to happen.'

'I know the rules, Jasper. This is a temporary arrangement. Besides, once it's over I might even take Myles back.' She knew this was completely untrue, but it would disarm Jasper, giving her a chance to recover her thoughts.

He stared at her with shock widening his eyes. 'You're surely not serious?'

'Why not?'

'Because he doesn't love you, that's why.'

'Nor do you.'

'That's completely beside the point,' he said. 'You can't possibly be thinking of tying yourself to a man who used you in such a despicable way.'

She gave him an ironic look. 'You know, your brother Raymond said almost the very same thing about you.'

His eyes narrowed in anger. 'I have at least been honest with you about my intentions,' he said. 'You knew the score when you agreed to marry me.'

'I really had very little choice in the matter, if you remember,' she said. 'You made it pretty clear I would suffer some rather unpleasant financial circumstances if I didn't agree to go along with your plans. I always knew you were a pretty ruthless sort of man but this time you took it to a whole new level.'

'Don't worry, you'll be more than adequately compensated for your trouble,' he said, turning to the mini bar and pouring himself a liqueur.

'But Duncan Brocklehurst said no money was to change hands,' she said. 'You're not supposed to pay me to be your wife.'

He tipped back his head and downed the contents of his

glass before he turned back to face her. 'There are other means of compensation other than money,' he said.

Hayley couldn't read his expression. It made her feel distinctly uneasy not knowing what he had planned.

'I suppose that's why you bought me such a flashy expensive engagement ring, was it?' she asked, 'A little consolation prize for agreeing to be your temporary wife, just like this expensive honeymoon, no doubt to make me think twice about asking for half of your assets when we divorce.'

His expression twisted in cynicism. 'That's really why you went ahead with it, wasn't it, Hayley? It wasn't about your finances at all. You could have got a temporary line of credit to tide you over if things had got tough. The truth is you wanted to marry me so you could take revenge for what happened when you were sixteen.'

Hayley felt her cheeks flame with shame as the memory of that night flooded her brain. He had humiliated her for attempting to seduce him, the dressing down he had given her had made her hate him for years. He was right in that she had agreed to marry him for revenge, but how could she tell him she had changed her mind?

'I know how your mind works, Hayley,' he continued. 'You're like a lot of other women I've had dealings with. One whiff of rejection and you're immediately after blood.'

'That's not true,' she said. 'I don't want anything from you, or at least not for myself.'

'I suppose I won't be able to test the truth of that statement until we file for divorce,' he said.

'You'll just have to wait and see, then, won't you?' she tossed back. 'But if I take anything off you I will give it straight to your son, who surely deserves it more than me.'

His expression became masklike. 'Have you ever met him?' he asked after a short but tense silence.

'No.'

'How well do you know Miriam Moorebank?'

She found it hard to hold his probing gaze. 'Not that well,' she admitted. 'She was a few years ahead of me at school so we weren't exactly close friends. I felt sorry for her after...after what happened. She was a bright student who had to give up everything because she chose to keep her baby.'

'It was her choice.'

Hayley frowned at the cool detachment of his tone. 'She could have done anything she liked, Jasper,' she said. 'She was a straight A student. Do you know what she does now?'

He didn't answer, but his expression told her he wasn't the least bit interested. That really annoyed her. How could he treat the mother of his child with such callousness?

'She cleans at a cheap, sleazy motel in the suburbs,' she informed him coldly. 'She could have done medicine or law for God's sake, and yet she cleans motel rooms for a living. Don't you feel even the tiniest bit guilty about that?'

His brown-black eyes met hers without flinching. 'No, I don't.'

Hayley felt her chest tighten with anger. How could he be so shallow and unfeeling? And, more to the point, how could she have fallen in love with such a man?

'How often do you see your son?' she asked.

'I see Daniel when he wants to see me,' he answered.

'How often is that?'

'It depends.'

'On what?'

'On whether he wants me to see him.'

'Do you actively seek to see him?' she asked. 'I mean whenever your busy, shallow, self-serving life allows you the time to do so.'

A flickering pulse of anger appeared at the edge of his mouth. 'If he wants to contact me he knows how to do so.'

'So you leave it up to him?'

'He's fifteen years old,' he said. 'If he wants contact with me, then that's surely up to him. I can't force it on him.'

'He's your flesh and blood! The teenage years are the hardest of all, particularly for boys. He needs you now more than ever.'

'I told you to stay out of my personal life, Hayley,' he said. 'My relationship with Daniel has nothing to do with you.'

'I'm your wife, for God's sake!'

His crooked smile had a hint of cruelty about it. 'Not for long,' he reminded her.

She drew herself up stiffly. 'You're counting, aren't you? Every day, every minute you're counting.'

'And you aren't?'

She sent him a furious glare. 'I'm counting the days until I can rid myself of your presence—permanently.'

He ran his dark gaze over her indolently. 'You seem to have enjoyed it so far.' He stepped towards her and lifted her chin, his fingers as hot as a brand on her skin. 'Who knows? You might even miss me when it's over.'

'I'm sure I won't.'

His mouth came down to within a breath of hers. 'I'd better make sure every minute of our marriage is truly memorable, then. What do you think, baby girl?'

Hayley couldn't think. That was the whole trouble. Not with his mouth so close and the temptation of his hard body burning its sexual promise against hers. She felt her eyelids flutter and then finally close as his mouth came down and sealed hers in a blistering kiss of passion. She felt his arms lift her as if she weighed...? Well, a whole lot less than she weighed, she thought a little wryly as he carried her to the huge bed.

She sighed with deep pleasure as she sank into the soft as

air mattress as his weight came down over her, his body pinning her beneath him, his mouth fused to hers, his hands already seeking the softness of her breasts. His warm palms shaped her through the thin fabric of her dress before he removed it over her head with an urgency that thrilled her, his dark, burning gaze feeding of her hungrily as she was finally naked before him. She sucked in her belly as his teeth surrounded her right nipple, the sexy graze arching her spine as he pulled on her almost savagely. She gave another ragged sigh of bliss as his head moved down her body until he came to the throbbing heart of her need, his tongue a hot, piercing sword of sensuality as he took her to heaven.

CHAPTER THIRTEEN

HAYLEY WOKE TO the warm brush of sunshine on her face and the heated press of Jasper's body at her back. She moved experimentally, not all that surprised when her inner muscles protested slightly when she shifted her legs against his.

His lovemaking of the night before had been breathtakingly satisfying. Her body felt as if it had been lifted to the heights of awareness, every nerve tingling in response to his mouth and hands and hard male presence. She had not thought herself capable of such wild abandonment. Even recalling his grunting pleasure as he took her from behind for the first time had her belly quivering all over again, especially now as she could feel him stirring between her legs.

'Are you awake?' he asked, kissing her neck.

She turned her head to look over her shoulder at him. 'Is that meant to be your idea of foreplay?'

He flipped her onto her back and, after quickly applying a condom, sank into her without preamble, his dark eyes glinting with amusement. 'I could feel you twitching and rubbing up against me for the last half-hour,' he said. 'Haven't you had enough of me yet?'

Never, Hayley thought as she looked into his smouldering gaze. She had given up denying her attraction towards him.

There didn't seem any point fighting it when all she wanted was to be in his arms for as long as he wanted her there.

'Haven't you had enough of me?' she turned his question around.

He pressed a bruising kiss to her mouth as he sank even deeper into her silky warmth, moving in and out slowly but tantalisingly. 'Not yet,' he said. 'I'm still discovering things about you.'

'What things?' she asked, running a fingertip over the arch of one of his dark brows, her body on fire as he thrust deeper.

He captured her hand and sucked on her fingertip for a moment before answering. 'I had no idea you talked in your sleep,' he said, his thumb rolling over the underside of her wrist as he held her gaze.

Hayley felt her stomach drop in alarm. What had she said? Had she inadvertently revealed her feelings towards him? 'What did I talk about?' she asked, trying her best not to sound too concerned.

'I'm not sure I should tell you.' His dark eyes twinkled. 'It might embarrass you.'

Twin pools of colour began to heat her cheeks. 'I was probably having a nightmare or something.'

He didn't elaborate, instead he picked up his pace until she was breathlessly trying to keep up, her body tightening around him, her senses spinning as he took her on a rollercoaster ride to paradise.

She floated back down to earth a few minutes later, her body slick with sweat.

Jasper eased himself away and, brushing back her hair off her face, pressed a kiss to the tip of her nose. 'Do you feel like going on a picnic?' he asked.

'Where to?'

'To a private beach,' he said. 'I've organised a gourmet picnic hamper. I'll pick it up while you have the first shower.'

Hayley soaped her body a few minutes later as the water cascaded down, her flesh tingling all over as she saw the bruise-like fingerprints on her thighs where Jasper had held her to receive his driving force. She shivered all over as she recalled the almost primal possession of his mouth on their tenderness. Her hands drifted to the seam of her body, the flesh still tender and swollen from his demanding lovemaking, her awareness of her femininity an awakening in itself. She felt like a priceless musical instrument that only his hands could play with such exquisite harmony.

She was dressed in a bikini and sarong and sandals when he came back with the picnic and they spent a glorious afternoon lazing on one of the private beaches, sipping wine and sharing the sumptuous feast.

Jasper had even stopped to pick up two stinger suits so they could swim and snorkel in the tropical water without fear of being stung by the deadly box jellyfish.

The afternoon drifted into evening, where after a fabulous dinner they sat together in the private spa, sipping even more champagne as they looked over the silver ocean below, its surface wrinkled by a light warm breeze.

Hayley gave a contented sigh as she stretched out her legs. 'I wish I could stay here for ever.'

His feet began to toy with hers beneath the bubbling water. 'With me?' he asked with a sexy smile.

She smiled back at him coyly. 'I suppose there could be worse people I could get stranded on a tropical island with.'

'I must have moved up on that list of yours,' he said, stroking her inner thigh with his foot. 'Wasn't I the last person on earth or something?'

She splashed some water at him, but he captured her hands and pulled her towards him so she was straddling him. Her breath halted when she felt the hot probe of his erection, her body instantly on fire.

His eyes locked down on hers. 'You know something, Hayley?'

'What?' she breathed raggedly as she gazed at his mouth as it came towards hers.

'I think it's been far too long since we last made love,' he said, brushing her mouth with his before adding, 'It's been about three hours at least.'

'You're right,' she said, her tongue darting out to flicker teasingly against his lips. 'So what do you suggest we do about it?'

His dark eyes glinted as he cupped her face in his hands. 'I was thinking something along the lines of this,' he said as he covered her mouth with his.

The next six days passed in a blur of blissful contentment as Hayley lapped up the luxury of the island paradise and the heady magic of being in Jasper's arms. Her body sang to the tune of his touch, her senses leaping whenever he looked at her with one of his lazy I-know-what-you're-thinking-about smiles. She couldn't help shivering with delight when she thought of the sensual heights she had scaled under his expert tuition, and in her darker moments wondered how she would live without such breathtaking excitement in the days to come. He hadn't mentioned the end of their marriage again; she didn't dare hope it was because he was having second thoughts about ending it at the agreed time. And in an effort to prolong the harmony they were sharing she mostly stayed clear of touchy subjects, trying to make the most of the time together so she could have some memories to keep that weren't tainted by their usual bitter bickering.

She found it surprising how much she enjoyed his company when she wasn't trying to score points off him. He seemed to relax as well, the shadows that lurked in his dark eyes gradually fading and the tension she'd grown used to seeing in his body visibly easing.

But to her dismay they had only just landed in Cairns to pick up the connecting flight back to Sydney when Hayley noticed a change in him. He had briefly turned his mobile on to check for messages and as he scrolled through them she saw a dark curtain come down over his features.

'Is everything all right?' she asked as he pocketed his phone with a frown.

'What?' he asked with an irritated edge to his tone as he looked down at her, as if he'd never seen her before and couldn't work out why she was standing there beside him.

'There's no need to bite my head off,' she said with an affronted toss of her head.

His hand scored a jagged pathway through his hair as he let out a sigh. 'Sorry, sweetheart,' he said with a quick on-off smile that didn't involve his eyes. 'I have some unexpected business to see to when I get back.'

'Do you want to talk to me about it?' she asked, linking her arm through his. 'Maybe I can help in some way.'

He looked down at her arm and gently but firmly removed it from his. 'Thanks, but no, thanks. I can manage. You have your own business to run without becoming involved in mine.'

Hayley felt her shoulders sag with disappointment. He was already shutting her out of his life. She followed him to the boarding gate but he was silent all the way back to Sydney, barely addressing a single comment to her, his expression pulled tight as if something deep inside him was gnawing at him.

His mood was no better when they arrived at his house. He prowled about like a caged lion, even snapping at her when she asked him what he wanted to do about dinner.

'For God's sake, Hayley, will you stop it with the loving-wife routine? You're driving me nuts being so nice.'

'Well, perhaps you'd like to move out now?' she said, folding her arms across her body. 'Why drag this out another three weeks when it's obvious you're already sick to death of me.'

He let out a hard-bitten expletive and reached for his keys. 'I'm going out,' he informed her tersely.

'Where are you going?'

'To see someone. Don't wait up.'

'I probably won't even be here when you get back,' she clipped out, desperately fighting back tears.

'That's entirely up to you, of course,' he said, and without another backward glance closed the door behind him.

Hayley seriously considered leaving right then and there, but she was tired and hungry and the thought of traipsing back to her flat with her things was suddenly all too difficult.

Instead she unpacked her things and did a load of washing before having a shower and a bite to eat…well, perhaps more than just a bite, she thought with a rueful grimace at the empty ice-cream tub as she stuffed it into the bin.

She watched television until her eyes began to glaze over, and looking at her watch, felt her insides twist when she saw it was almost three a.m. Jasper hadn't returned and, recalling the text message he'd received, she couldn't help wondering if one of his many lovers had arranged a late night assignation with him. Her blood boiled at the thought of him cavorting with another woman so soon after marrying her. In spite of the temporary nature of their marriage, it still hurt unbearably to think he cared so little for her feelings that he would openly betray the intimacy they had shared over the last week.

She trudged despondently off to bed, choosing to sleep in the spare room to send him a very clear message of what she thought of his behaviour, but in the end her message went unnoticed as he didn't return at all.

Hayley came downstairs bleary-eyed the next morning to find a tiny middle-aged Filipino woman bustling about the kitchen, her enthusiastic greeting when she saw Hayley doing a power of good to her battered self-esteem, even though the housekeeper's rapid speech left some things lost in translation.

'My name is Rosario,' she said. 'You his wife, ah so beautiful! You happy girl, eh? He very good in the bedroom, yes?' Her eyes twinkled mischievously.

'Um…er…' Hayley faltered, trying not to blush.

'Would you like breakfast? I make good breakfast for you. Sit down. Would you like cup of coffee?'

Hayley sat down and lapped up the attention. Rosario chatted non-stop but she didn't mind—it was a relief not to have to contribute more than a 'yes' or 'no' or 'oh, really' now and again.

'He very good boss,' the housekeeper said as she cleared away the breakfast things a little while later. 'He pay me good money. He very kind.'

'Yes.'

'He need a good wife now. Time to settle down and have lots of babies, eh?'

Hayley smiled a little weakly without responding.

'You a nice girl,' Rosario said. 'I can see that. You don't love him for his money, not like all the others. He work too hard. I always tell him he should relax but he not listen to me. But you will be good for him. You love him very much, eh?' Rosario clapped her hands together in delight. 'This will be very good marriage. I know it.'

Hayley felt her heart tighten painfully. All of a sudden she realized that quite possibly she had been in love with Jasper since she was sixteen. How could she tell the cheerful little housekeeper that the marriage was not only not good—it was going to be over in twenty-three days?

Lucy greeted Hayley warmly when she came into the salon later that morning. 'So how did the pretend honeymoon go?'

'It was…good…'

Lucy's finely arched brows rose slightly. 'You didn't do it with him, did you?'

Hayley averted her gaze as she inspected the appointment book. 'Do what?'

'You know what. Slept with him. Had sex. Got down and dirty with him.'

'So what if I did?'

Lucy groaned. 'I knew you wouldn't be able to help yourself. God, Hayley, are you crazy or something? It's not a real marriage. He's going to move on as soon as he can.'

Hayley swivelled her gaze to look at her friend. 'I thought you were starting to like him? You said he was a big improvement on Myles.'

'I do like him, what woman wouldn't? He's charm and hot sex personified but it doesn't mean you should have taken things that far with him.'

Hayley let out a heartfelt sigh. 'I know, but I just couldn't help it.'

'Don't tell me you've fallen in love with him. That would be about the stupidest thing you've ever done.'

Hayley didn't answer.

'*Shoot*, Hayley,' Lucy said. 'You have, haven't you?'

'I know it's stupid and crazy and all of those things, but I've loved him for years.'

'So why were you planning to marry Myles if you really loved Jasper?'

Hayley gave her a rueful look. 'That was another stupid and

crazy thing I did. You were right when you said you thought I was looking for security. I think I knew deep down I could never have Jasper so I settled on second best.'

'But you've got Jasper now, albeit temporarily,' Lucy commented.

'Yes.'

'So what are you going to do?'

'I don't know…stick it out, pray for a miracle, and hope he falls in love with me.'

'But what if he doesn't?' Lucy asked, her expression full of concern. 'He's not good marriage material, Hayley. His little black book is not little—it's the size of an encyclopedia. He's already left one woman in the lurch. I couldn't bear to see that happen to you.'

'I'll be fine.'

'You are on the pill, aren't you?' Lucy asked. 'You sorted out that trouble with the last one you were trying didn't you?'

'Um…yes…that's all sorted.'

Lucy pursed her lips thoughtfully. 'And you've been using condoms, right?'

'Mostly.'

'What do you mean "mostly"? For God's sake, Hayley, Jasper Caulfield's been around more blocks than a New York city cab driver.'

'I know what I'm doing,' Hayley said. 'If anything…happens I'll have to face it alone. I know that. I've always known that.'

Lucy gave her a big squishy hug. 'Just be careful, Hayley. I don't want to see you get your heart smashed to pieces. Look what happened to Miriam Moorebank. It was years before she found a nice guy to marry her. Men don't like women with the sort of baggage that wears nappies.'

How could I forget? Hayley thought in sinking despair.

CHAPTER FOURTEEN

WHEN JASPER CAME home that evening Hayley was waiting for him in the lounge.

'Where did you go last night?' she asked.

'I told you I had some business to see to,' he said as he poured himself a drink.

She found his cool, offhand manner immensely irritating and threw him a scornful glare. *'All night?'*

He took a sip of his brandy before answering. 'Yes, as a matter of fact.'

Her blue-green eyes flashed with sparks of anger. 'You're a lying, cheating bastard,' she spat. 'Who were you with?'

'I don't have to discuss my private affairs with you.'

'Affairs is exactly the right term, isn't it, Jasper? You just can't help yourself, can you? One woman is never enough for you.'

'You are acting like a jealous wife, Hayley. I warned you about getting too attached to the role.'

'Don't worry. I know we've only got twenty-three days left. But let me tell you something for free. If you think you can go out all night, then so can I, and, like you, I won't tell you where I've gone or who I've been with.'

His mouth tightened as he set his glass down. 'You wouldn't.'

She lifted her chin. 'You just watch me, sweetheart,' she said and flounced out of the room.

Hayley hadn't really intended going out at all, but when he didn't call her back or even follow her out of the room she decided she would just for the heck of it. She scooped up her purse and keys and left, but once she was on her way down the street she really had no idea where to go until she drove past the hotel she and Myles had often gone to for a pre-dinner drink while they had been dating. She pulled into the arrival bay and left her car with the parking valet attendant and went inside.

She sat in the piano bar sipping a fruity mocktail, trying not to blubber over the mournful songs being played. She was onto her second drink and her last tissue when a voice called out to her in surprise.

'Hayley!'

'Myles,' she said, inwardly groaning.

He took the seat opposite. 'What are you doing here all by yourself? Where's your husband?'

'Um…he'll be along shortly,' she lied.

He took her hand before she could stop him. 'Hayley, I feel terrible about what happened. I want you to know I've completely finished with paying for…well, you know.'

'It's all right, Myles,' she said, trying to remove her hand from his.

'No,' Myles said, his grip on her hand tightening. 'I love you, Hayley. I hurt you abominably. I've been agonising over it for the past week or so. I want you to know that if things don't work out with Jasper Caulfield I will be here for you. We can run away together, have the baby as we planned. We can set ourselves up for life with the money you get from the divorce.'

'Myles, *please*—'

A tall shadow fell over her as a deep voice drawled, 'How very touching.'

Hayley pulled her hand away from Myles's and got unsteadily to her feet. 'Jasper…I…I…' It was pointless going on, she decided. The blistering look he was giving her informed her she would be wasting her time trying to dig herself out of this particular hole.

Jasper turned to Myles. 'If you will excuse us, Lederman,' he said with a supercilious smile. 'My wife and I have some important business to attend to. I hope you understand.'

'Yes…yes, of course,' Myles said, looking flustered.

Hayley felt the savage bite of Jasper's fingers around her wrist as he led her from the hotel, her feet almost tripping over themselves as he gave no consideration to her much shorter stride.

He handed the parking valet attendant a wad of cash and gave him instructions on where to have Hayley's car delivered, his face rigid with anger as he led her to his own car.

'Get in,' he barked at her as he wrenched open the door.

Hayley got in and he snapped the door shut and strode around to the driver's side, his expression thunderous as he started the car with a bellowing roar.

'Jasper, I—'

'Leave it,' he cut her off tersely. 'I don't want to hear any of your bare-faced lies.'

'But you don't understand—'

'I understand what you're up to, Hayley. I've suspected it from the start. You could have easily got out of marrying me in spite of the pressure I put on you, but you didn't because you wanted a chance to get revenge and what better way than the way your mother did to my father?'

'That's not true,' she said. 'It was at first, I admit, but not now.'

'I suppose you're going to say you've fallen in love with me just to dig the dagger in a bit harder, aren't you?' he accused. 'But don't waste your breath. You might be a great lay, sweetheart, but that's all you're getting from me and only for another few days.'

Anger came to her shattered pride's rescue. 'I don't want anything from you,' she said. 'You're a cold, unfeeling bastard and I hope you rot in hell.'

He drove the rest of the way back to his house in a simmering silence, his expression so dark with fury she felt a flicker of fear deep inside her belly.

Once inside the house she made to go up the stairs but he caught her arm on the way past and pulled her back to face him. 'Not so fast, baby girl. I haven't finished with you yet.'

She slapped at his hand. 'I have nothing to say to you.'

'I wasn't thinking along the lines of conversation,' he said, pulling her close to his hard body, his eyes glittering with sexual heat. 'What about it, sugar? Want to make the most of this marriage while it lasts?'

Hayley tried not to look at the sensual curve of his mouth and looked into his dark, smouldering gaze instead. But that was an even bigger mistake. She felt the magnetic pull, the force of attraction too strong to resist as his mouth came crashing down on hers. It was a kiss of turbulent, out-of-control emotions; anger, passion, frustration and frantic need were all there in a cataclysmic combination that threatened to unravel her completely. His tongue delved between her lips like a torpedo on a search and destroy mission, each swoop and thrust rendering her boneless in his crushing hold.

His hands pushed away the straps of her dress with rough urgency until he found her smooth naked form, her nipples so tight they drove their rosy points into his palms as he cupped her. His mouth left hers to take each peak between his teeth in a grazing action that was both painful and pleasurable until he opened his mouth over her and sucked on her hard. She whimpered at the abrasion of his tongue, the hot pull of his mouth making her toes curl in delight.

He turned her around, lifting her dress to her waist, his body probing her from behind with an eroticism she could barely withstand. Her whole body trembled with anticipation as he shoved her knickers to one side, the rasp of his zip sending her heart rate soaring.

'Oh, *yes...*' she gasped breathlessly as he drove into her silken warmth, burying himself so deeply she could feel him against the neck of her womb.

The pace he set carried her along with him on a roller-coaster ride of nerve-tingling ecstasy until she was sobbing out her release, her body convulsing with rapture as he burst inside her with a grunt of deep satisfaction.

He withdrew and turned her around and kissed her hard on the mouth, his hands cupping her face for a moment before he finally released her.

She stood uncertainly before him, her body still tingling from the scorch of his touch. 'Jasper?'

He turned and zipped up his trousers, his hand scoring a rough pathway through the thickness of his hair as he moved to the other side of the room, his back like an impenetrable wall.

Hayley wasn't a hundred per cent sure, but she suspected he was as deeply affected by their lovemaking as she was. The expression she had seen pass so fleetingly over his face was one of startled bewilderment, as if he had never experienced something so powerful or so totally consuming before.

'I know you probably won't believe me, Jasper, but I didn't plan to meet Myles this evening.'

He turned around to face her, his expression tight with cynicism. 'You're right. I don't believe you.'

'I mean it, Jasper. I wouldn't betray you like that. I don't feel anything for Myles, in fact I wonder now if I ever did.'

'I'm not interested, Hayley,' he said, retrieving his mobile phone from his back pocket as it began to beep with a message tone. He looked down at the screen, a heavy frown bringing his brows almost together.

'I suppose that's another one of your lovers looking for you, is it?' she asked before she could stop herself. 'You're such a hypocrite dragging me back here acting like a jealous husband just because I happened to innocently run into my ex-fiancé when you bed hop more than a bedbug. But then I'm just your temporary wife. Why should I care if you go from me to her?'

His eyes met hers for a brief moment, the hardness in their chocolate-brown depths sending an arrow right through her heart. 'That's right, Hayley,' he said. 'Why should you care?'

Because I damn well love you, that's why. The words were on her tongue and just about to spill out, but before she could open her mouth he had turned and left, the door snapping shut behind him with a chilling finality.

Hayley was well aware over the next two weeks that Jasper was doing his best to avoid her. She threw herself into work at the salon, pinning a bright smile on her face for the sake of her clients, but as she drove back to Jasper's house each evening it was with a heavy heart.

She had moved her things back into one of the spare rooms, and when Rosario gave her a puzzled look when she came to clean Hayley explained she had a cold and didn't want to give it to Jasper. It was partly true, she rationalised the little white lie. She did feel unwell. Her appetite had faded considerably, which was highly unusual, and her stomach felt squeamish every time she smelt certain aromas, in particular coffee.

The following day Lucy came from the café down the road with their standard mid-morning pick-me-up caffeine hit.

'One latte coming up,' she said and, taking off the lid, handed it to her.

Hayley put a hand up to her mouth and ran out the back to the small bathroom and promptly threw up. Lucy squeezed in behind her and handed her a soft towel.

'I'm thinking that instead of the coffee maybe I should have bought you a pregnancy test instead,' she remarked wryly.

Hayley felt her skin begin to shiver as she did the numbers on her cycle. She was ten days late, which was not all that unusual as she had never been particularly regular, especially during times of stress, but her breasts were feeling tender as well. She had been pushing the thought aside for days, unwilling to accept the possibility that she was carrying Jasper's child. A child he would see as a mistake just like the first one he had fathered.

'It might be a stomach bug,' she said in between another bout of retching.

'Yeah, I've seen that type of bug before. It lasts about nine months and grows to the size of a small football,' Lucy said dryly.

Hayley washed her face and grimaced as she looked in the mirror. 'It would be just my luck. We're splitting up in a week.'

'So he's still pretty keen to call an end to it?' Lucy asked.

Hayley sighed. 'Yes. He's already distancing himself. I can feel it.'

'I won't say I told you so.'

'Thanks.'

'But I will say why don't you take the rest of the day off? I've had a cancellation so I can do Mrs Pritchard for you and the rest of the day's bookings are fairly well spaced.'

'Would you mind?'

'Of course not,' Lucy said with a smile. 'Go and get a test done and have a think about what you're going to do.'

'I already know what I'm going to do,' Hayley said as she gathered her things together.

Lucy gave her a penetrating look. 'You're not thinking of not telling him, are you?'

'I can't tell him.'

'You *have* to tell him!'

'No, Lucy. I can't. Do you realise how angry he would be? He's had to deal with an unwanted child ever since he was eighteen. I couldn't possibly tell him, he might make me have an abortion or something.'

'No one can force you to do that unless you think it's the right thing for you.'

'It wouldn't be the right thing for me, but telling Jasper he's going to be a father is not going to be the right thing either. He'll think I did it deliberately to trap him into staying married to me.'

'Didn't you?'

Hayley bit her lip. 'Not consciously, but maybe deep down inside I think I let things happen that shouldn't have happened,' she confessed. 'I should have been more careful.'

'It seems to me even a nun would have a hard time resisting Jasper Caulfield,' Lucy said as she rinsed out the towel and handed it to Hayley.

'Tell me about it,' Hayley said as she buried her head into its cooling freshness.

Hayley looked at the results of the pregnancy test with a combination of joy and dread. She put a hand to her belly and felt a wave of awe pass through her that she was carrying Jasper's child. But when she allowed herself to think of his reaction to the news she felt a tidal wave of panic swamp her. Her only comfort was they would be soon separating and unlikely to run into each other now that Gerald had passed away. It was against her principles to conceal such life-changing news from him but she knew he had no interest in being a father a second time.

She heard him come home and quickly scrunched up the packet and stuffed it in the bottom of the bathroom bin, promising herself she'd take it out to the main rubbish container later.

She stayed in the spare room, assuming he would go out as he had done every night for the last two weeks, but instead she heard his footsteps stop outside her door.

'Hayley, I'd like a word with you.'

She got off the bed and tentatively opened the door. 'Yes?'

His gaze swept over her pale face and disordered hair. 'Are you OK?'

'Of course…I'm just a bit tired, that's all.'

'Well, I guess that more or less answers my question without even asking it,' he said.

'What did you want to ask me?'

'I was wondering if you wanted to have dinner with me this evening,' he said.

Hayley hid her secret delight behind sarcasm. 'Have you run out of alternative dates?' she asked.

'No, but I have a work function tonight and I thought you might like to join me.'

Her delight swiftly turned to anger. 'So the only reason you're asking me is because you need me to play the role of devoted new wife.'

'That is one of the reasons, yes, but there's another one.'

'Which is?'

He seemed to hesitate before he answered. 'I realise I've been uncommunicative lately. It's hardly fair to take it out on you. I'm sorry but I've had a lot on my mind.'

Hayley knew she was being a fool for allowing herself to be mollified by his uncharacteristic apology, but she felt her defences melting all the same. 'Do you want to talk about it?' she asked.

He brushed her chin with the back of his knuckles, the touch so soft she felt as if her heart had swelled to twice its size. 'How soon can you get ready?' he asked.

She put a hand to her hair and grimaced. 'I need to have a shower and put some make-up on.'

'I'll give you fifteen minutes.'

The dinner was held in a restaurant overlooking Bondi Beach and even with the lively chatter and clinking of glasses and rattling of cutlery Hayley could still hear the sea pounding against the shore below.

She was seated on Jasper's left next to a man in his late thirties who owned a construction company that Jasper used for some of his larger projects.

'I must say I was surprised but delighted to hear about your marriage to Jasper,' Dave Braithwaite said. 'I've been telling him for years he needs to settle down and have a couple of kids.'

'Are you married?' Hayley asked, conscious of Jasper's arm draped along the back of her chair.

'Yep, been married ten years now. My wife, Anna, would be here tonight except she's expecting our third child. She's been having bouts of morning, midday and afternoon and evening sickness, poor darling.'

Hayley felt a hot blush move up from her toes to pool in her cheeks. 'I hope she feels better soon,' she said, shivering when Jasper's fingers wove their way into her hair at the back of her neck.

'So how about it, old boy?' Dave addressed Jasper by leaning in front of Hayley. 'Don't you think Hayley would make a beautiful mother? You don't want to leave it too long.

Have your kids while you're still young enough to keep up with them.'

Hayley felt the tension in Jasper's fingers and answered for him with a forced laugh. 'We've only been married just over three weeks. Give us time.'

Dave grinned. 'My eldest child, Julie, was conceived on our honeymoon. Never once regretted it either. She's an angel, so too is my son, Ben. Kids make you complete; there's nothing like seeing your children born. I haven't cried since I was a kid, but I howled like an idiot when they came into the world.'

Jasper's attention was called away by the person sitting on the right and Hayley felt her shoulders sink in relief. She chatted a little longer to Dave about his children before politely excusing herself when she saw the waiter approaching with coffee.

Jasper found her standing on the balcony of the restaurant a short time later, the sea breeze lifting the curly strands of her hair. 'Are you all right?' he asked.

'Yes, of course.' She forced a bright smile to her lips. 'I just felt like some fresh air.'

'I'm sorry about Dave,' he said. 'He's a bit full on at times.'

'I thought he was nice.'

He looked down at her, his dark eyes suddenly intense in the subdued lighting. 'Hayley…'

'Yes?' She kicked herself for answering so quickly and with such pathetic hopefulness in her tone.

His dark, unfathomable eyes held hers for endless moments.

'I'm sorry to do this to you, but I have to see someone tonight on an urgent matter,' he said.

She swallowed against the disappointment rising from deep within her. 'I see.'

'I don't know when I'll be back. I just got a call a moment ago.'

'Was it from a woman?' The question burst out before she could stop it.

She saw the answer in his eyes before they moved away from hers. 'It's not what you think, Hayley,' he said heavily.

'Spare me the sordid details.'

He took her arm. 'Come on, I'll drive you home.'

She pulled out of his hold and sent him a glittering glare. 'Please don't go out of your way. I'd hate to keep you from your terribly important late night business. I'll get a cab.'

Jasper watched her stalk back into the restaurant, but he didn't have time to call her back, even though he wished to God he could explain.

CHAPTER FIFTEEN

HAYLEY WAS JUST thinking about going to bed about an hour later when she heard the front entrance intercom chime signalling someone was seeking entry. She tied her wrap a little tighter around her middle, and, going to the intercom panel on the wall, asked who was there.

'It's Daniel,' a young male voice said.

She activated the security system and opened the door to see a tall gangly teenager with mid-brown hair walking up the pathway. As he came even further into the light her gaze immediately went to the blue-black bruise covering his right eye and then to his cut and swollen bottom lip.

'Oh, my God!' she gasped. 'What on earth happened to you?'

He shifted from foot to foot in an awkward and self-conscious manner, his hazel eyes falling away from hers. 'I'm fine,' he mumbled. 'It looks much worse than it is.'

She ushered him in and closed the door. 'I'm Hayley, by the way,' she introduced herself. 'You must be Jasper's son, Daniel Moorebank.'

His eyes met hers briefly, something in their brown-green depths suggesting to her that he wasn't entirely comfortable with being identified as such.

'Is he home?' he asked after a slight but telling pause.

'No, I'm sorry,' she said. 'He had some…er…business to see to.'

'Do you know when he'll be back?'

Hayley felt a bit of a fool for not being able to give him a straight answer. 'I'm not sure, Daniel. He didn't put a time on it. But why don't you stay and let me put some ice on your eye? It looks terribly sore.'

'I don't want to be a bother…' He shuffled from foot to foot again, his thin shoulders slightly hunched.

Hayley pulled out a chair for him. 'Here, sit yourself down and I'll get an ice-pack. I'm sure your dad has one in the freezer somewhere. I think I saw it when I had some ice cream the other day.'

She came back with it wrapped in a hand towel and handed it to him. 'Just hold it against your eye for a while to take the swelling down,' she said. 'Would you like a glass of orange juice or something?'

His thin cheeks flushed with colour. 'I shouldn't even be here,' he said with a downturn of his mouth.

She took the chair opposite. 'Of course you should come here whenever you want to,' she said. 'You have every right to see your father.'

His eyes came back to hers momentarily before shifting away again. 'I don't think of him that way… He's always been just Jasper to me.'

She frowned at him. 'You don't call him Dad?'

He shook his head. 'It wouldn't be appropriate. We don't have that sort of relationship.'

Hayley felt her hackles rising over the way Jasper had treated his only child. How had it come to this? The boy was obviously deeply troubled, his face looked as if he'd been in some sort of nasty scuffle and his whole demeanour was dejected and downtrodden. She knew enough about young men to know they needed good role models in their life. Daniel was obviously a casualty of Jasper's neglect to follow through on his responsibilities as a father.

'Does your mother know where you are?' she asked into the silence.

A mask came over his face that instantly reminded her of Jasper. 'I told her I was going to a friend's house.'

'Would you like to stay here tonight?' Hayley asked on an impulse she couldn't restrain in time.

His lowered the ice-pack to look at her with both eyes. 'Would that be all right?' he asked, his expression touchingly hopeful, making him look a whole lot younger than his fifteen years.

'Of course it will be all right,' she assured him. 'Haven't you ever stayed over before?'

He shook his head and reapplied the ice pack to his eye. 'It wasn't really encouraged,' he said.

Hayley felt her anger towards Jasper hit an all time high. No doubt he didn't want his son hanging about when he brought his various lovers home to seduce the way he had seduced her, she thought resentfully. She gritted her teeth and determined that it was all going to change now…well, for the short time she was here at least.

'Have you had dinner?' she asked.

'No.'

'Would you like an omelette or a toasted sandwich or something?' she asked. 'It won't take me a minute or two to rustle one up for you.'

He gave her a grateful glance. 'If you're sure it's not too much trouble.'

She sprang to her feet and pushed her chair in. 'It's no trouble at all. I love cooking. I also love eating, which is a bit of a downside really.'

He gave her a lopsided smile on account of his lip. 'I don't think you have too much to worry about. Jasper told me you had a fabulous figure.'

She gaped at him in surprise. 'He told you that?'

'Yes.' He paused for a moment before adding, 'I'm sorry I couldn't come to your wedding. I wanted to but…'

'I understand,' she said, wondering what Jasper had told his son about the circumstances leading to their marriage.

'I think it's great Jasper's going to settle down at last,' Daniel continued. 'I've always felt a bit guilty that it was because of me that he shied away from marriage for this long.'

'I'm sure that's not true,' she said, even though she knew for a fact it was.

Daniel looked at her again. 'I don't think anyone should be forced to do something they don't want to do,' he said. 'It would have been a disaster…you know…him marrying my mum.'

Hayley turned her attention to cracking eggs into a bowl. 'What makes you say that?' she asked.

'He doesn't love her. He has never loved her.'

He doesn't love me either, Hayley felt like saying. She turned around, the bowl still in her hands as she faced him. 'But he cares for you,' she said. 'And you care for him, don't you?'

Daniel's expression visibly softened. 'He's the best friend a guy could ever ask for. I don't think there's a person I care more about than Jasper. He's the reason I've coped for this long.'

Hayley felt as if she'd missed something somewhere. What was he talking about? Coped with what? She put the bowl down and turned on the cook top, busying herself with the task of making him a meal, her mind twisting and turning as she tried to make sense of his contradictory statements.

'You and Jasper lived at Crickglades together for a couple of years, didn't you?' Daniel was the first to break the small silence.

She checked on the omelette before turning to look at him. 'Yes. I moved in when I was fourteen. I left after the divorce three years later.'

'I guess that's why I haven't met you before—out at Crickglades, I mean,' he said.

'Did you see much of your grandfather Gerald?' she asked.

'Now and again,' he said with a hint of regret. 'Not as much as I would have liked.'

'It wasn't encouraged?' She took a wild guess.

He gave her a twisted smile. 'Yeah, something like that.'

She turned back to the omelette and deftly slid it onto a plate and handed it to him. 'Well you're very welcome here—any time,' she said with a warm smile.

'Thanks,' he said, his cheeks flushing in a way that for once didn't remind her of Jasper.

Daniel had been in bed for at least an hour when Hayley heard Jasper return. She felt rather than heard his car, the grumbling roar of its engine reminding her of a lion returning to its lair. She could almost tell his mood from the deep, throaty growl as he killed the engine, the slam of the driver's door audible even in the lounge where she was sitting on the edge of one of the leather sofas waiting for him.

He came in, tossing his keys to the nearest surface with a muttered curse, his fists clenching and unclenching until he swung around and saw her.

Hayley's eyes flared in concern when she saw the cut on his lip that was still bleeding. 'Oh, my God! What on earth happened to you?' she asked for the second time that evening.

He wiped at his mouth with the back of his hand, grimacing

as he saw the smear of blood. 'It's nothing. It looks much worse than it is.'

The irony was remarkable, she thought as she came over to inspect the damage. 'You sound exactly like your son,' she said.

His whole body stiffened and a deep frown divided his forehead. 'Has he been here?' he asked.

'He *is* here,' she answered. 'He's asleep upstairs and looking very much like he ran into the same door you did.'

Jasper's expression soured even further. 'Yeah, well, it's a pretty solid door, but I think I've put it out of action for a while.'

She frowned up at him in confusion. 'What's going on?' she asked. 'Both you and Daniel turn up looking like you've done ten rounds with a heavyweight champion.'

Jasper pulled out his handkerchief and spat the blood out of his mouth before he answered. 'Stay out of it, Hayley. It's nothing to do with you.'

'No, I will not stay out of it. Tell me what the hell is going on. I have a right to know, if not as your wife then as a concerned third party. How could I not be concerned when a young boy of fifteen comes here with a black eye and a swollen lip?' she said.

'It's no concern of yours.'

She sent him an accusing look. 'Did *you* hit him?'

He jerked back from her as if she had slapped him, his face almost white with shock. 'How can you ask that?'

It was a pretty stupid question, she had to admit. Daniel had done nothing but praise his father the whole time she had been speaking to him. 'I'm sorry,' she mumbled. 'Of course you wouldn't do something like that.'

'What sort of man do you think I am?' he railed at her. 'He's a bloody kid, for God's sake. He's got enough on his plate right now without me cuffing him around the ears.'

Hayley watched as he strode to the drinks cabinet and poured himself a measure of spirits, downing it in one swallow, his hands visibly shaking as he gripped the glass when he set it back down.

'I'm sorry,' she said again. 'I was worried, that's all. He seems a nice kid. He reminds me of you.'

He swung around to look at her, his expression distinctly ironic. 'Does he? In what way?'

Her brow wrinkled as she thought about it for a moment. 'He's reserved, sort of private in a way. He doesn't like to wear his heart on his sleeve.'

'And you think that I'm like that?'

'I think you don't feel comfortable being vulnerable.'

'So you think I'm nice as well, do you?'

'I think you like people to think you're a tough guy but underneath you have feelings, you just don't like to have them on show,' she said.

He dabbed at his lip again. 'What feelings have you uncovered, baby girl?' he asked with a mocking edge to his tone.

'You love Daniel; I know you do.'

'I have never said I don't.'

'His stepfather appears to believe differently,' she said, recalling again Mrs Beckforth's comments.

'And you believe that jerk's account, do you?'

Hayley didn't know what to believe. She was becoming increasingly confused. Daniel and Jasper's relationship was hard to figure out. 'I can only go on what I'm told,' she said. 'And you tell me nothing, so what else can I believe?'

His mouth tightened, making his lip ooze more blood. He swiped at it angrily as he glared down at her. 'I told you to stay out of my affairs,' he said. 'This has nothing to do with you. It's between Miriam and Daniel and I.'

'That's not true,' she argued. 'I might only be a temporary wife but I care about you. I care about Daniel too.'

'You've only just met him. How can you possibly feel anything for him?'

'I *do* care about him,' she insisted. 'And I care about you. I love you. There, I've said it. I love you. I think I always have.'

His expression grew as tight as a closed fist. 'You're talking rubbish as usual. You're looking for security but I'm not the one to give it to you. You know the rules, Hayley. As soon as possible we'll be divorcing.'

'I don't want a divorce.'

His whole body froze as if she had just sprayed him with quick-setting concrete. 'But I do,' he said in a chillingly hard tone.

Tears sprang to her eyes. 'I know you don't mean that,' she choked. 'You're pushing me away because I've come too close. I know you, Jasper. I *know* you.'

'You're confusing sexual compatibility with something else.'

'So you admit we're compatible?' she asked.

'I can hardly deny it. As I said the other day you're a great lay, sweetheart, but as to a future together—forget it.'

She blinked back the bitter tears. 'I can't believe you're throwing away this chance at a life together. We could be so happy together, Jasper. I know we could.'

'For how long?'

'For ever.'

He gave a grunt of cynicism. 'You've been watching too many romantic movies. It doesn't work in the real world. Besides, you want different things out of life. You want kids and I don't.'

'But why not?' she asked, trying to ignore the tight clench of despair gripping her stomach. 'From what I've seen so far Daniel is a son to be proud of. He speaks so highly of you. He called you his best friend. How could you not want to experience that again, perhaps with a daughter or another son?'

'Because I've seen what it can do to a kid when parents separate or divorce,' he said bitterly. 'For years I've lain awake at night worrying if I did the right thing by Daniel. I don't want to have that on my conscience ever again.'

Hayley felt his pain like an electric current in the air. She had judged him so wrongly, accusing him of not caring about his son when the truth was he cared too much to damage Daniel's life as he had been damaged by his parents' bitter divorce. No wonder he had resisted marrying Miriam, especially at such a young age, in spite of the pressure put on him to do so. She was well aware of the statistics as he would have been too; teenage marriages rarely lasted the distance and the children of such early unions were nearly always the casualties.

'But you did do the right thing by Daniel,' she said softly. 'I didn't realise it before, but you've been there for him all this time.'

'But not in the way he needs,' he said as he poured himself another drink, wincing slightly as the alcohol stung the cut on his lip. 'I haven't been able to protect him.'

Hayley came over and took the glass out of his hand, her fingers curling around his as she looked into his dark, shadowed gaze. 'What do you mean?' she asked.

His eyes began to flash with hatred. 'His stepfather is an absolute bastard to him.'

Hayley felt her stomach clench in anguish. 'You mean he's…' she stumbled over the word '…violent towards him?'

He gave her a grim look. 'I'm probably going to have to ward off an assault charge after this evening, but it will be worth it.'

'You got into a fight with Miriam's husband?'

'I didn't throw the first punch, but I sure as hell wanted to,' he ground out.

'Is that what the phone call at the restaurant was about?' she asked.

'Miriam rang me to tell me Daniel had run away,' he said through clenched teeth. 'She's been covering up for that violent bastard. She was too frightened to say anything in case he took it out on Daniel.'

Hayley stared at him in shock. 'Why didn't you tell me this before?'

'I told you it's none of your business. It's my mess—I have to deal with it.'

'You can't keep shutting people out of your life, Jasper. How long has this been going on between Daniel and his step-father?'

'I didn't know anything about it until recently,' he said. 'Daniel too was trying to keep it quiet. I guess he felt he should be able to handle it on his own.'

'He's just a kid,' she said, frowning. 'He shouldn't have to cope with that sort of stuff. No one should.'

'He only told me because of the threats Martin made.'

'Threats?' Her eyes widened. 'What sort of threats?'

Jasper gave himself a mental kick. He had come way too close to letting the truth out, which reminded him all over again of how dangerous it was to let Hayley slip under his radar the way she had. He hadn't intended things to go this far but somehow she had wormed her way into his emotional no-go area. It was going to take a massive effort on his part to get her out but he was determined to do it.

'Bribes over money, that sort of thing,' he said, which was as close to the truth as he could comfortably get.

'I'm sorry for misjudging you, Jasper,' she said. 'I've spent most of my adult life criticising you, so I don't blame you for not trusting me now, but I do love you. I even wonder if Gerald suspected what my feelings were the last time I visited him.

Looking back now I seem to remember he wasn't all that impressed when I announced my engagement to Myles. I put it down to the fact that he was feeling so poorly, but now I can't help feeling he didn't approve and set to work to make it difficult for me to go ahead with the marriage, rewriting the will at the last minute. I think he wanted me to marry you. He wanted me to teach you how to love and trust again.'

Jasper put his hands on her shoulders, but instead of pushing her away as he'd intended, he brought her into his chest, burying his face in the fragrant cloud of her hair. 'I wish I could give you what you need, Hayley,' he said. 'But I can't risk ruining any more lives.'

She pulled back so she could look at him. 'Do you feel anything for me?' she asked, her blue-green eyes bright with moisture. 'Anything at all?'

He felt something rough and hard lodge in his throat and swallowed against it. 'I feel a lot of things, baby girl,' he said, blocking the pathway of one crystal tear with the pad of his thumb as it rolled down her cheek.

'Are you going to tell me what they are?'

He looked down into her beautiful face and wondered if he should tell her the truth about Miriam Moorebank. It might help her to understand his motivations, but then he reasoned it wouldn't really change anything in the long run. The fewer people who knew the truth, the better, especially at this delicate stage; Daniel had enough to deal with without any last minute complications.

He leaned down and pressed a kiss to the middle of her forehead. 'You deserve better than this, sweetheart. You really do.'

'But I only want you,' she insisted. 'I don't care for how long, just let me love you. Please?'

He sighed as she pressed herself into him, her softer

contours against his harder ones making his blood instantly quicken. God, how he wanted her! Was this hot rush of desire never going to go away? He had thought it would have run its course by now, but instead each time he drove himself inside her he felt another tight little gear shift in his chest.

'Please, Jasper,' she whispered as she brought her mouth to his, the gentle stroke of her tongue salving his swollen lip in an achingly intimate gesture that made speech difficult and thought impossible.

He swept her up into his arms and carried her to his bedroom, kicking the door shut with his foot before laying her on the bed. He looked at her with desire burning in his eyes as he tore the clothes off his body, his heart rate going through the roof when he watched her begin to remove her own clothes. She did it with teasing slowness, each movement of her hands making him nearly explode with fierce, out-of-control longing. She cupped her naked breasts and sent him a come-and-get-me look that made his scalp lift in anticipation.

There was no time for preliminaries, he was inside her and thrusting hard and urgently, her slippery warmth gripping him tightly, her gasping cries and panting breaths making him swell with male pride that he could bring her to such a point so quickly. She convulsed around him, her hips undulating under the rocking pressure of his, her mouth opening on a high cry of pleasure that he blocked with the flat of his palm in case Daniel could hear them.

'Shh, sweetheart,' he said. 'You'll wake up the neighbourhood, not to mention Daniel down the hall.'

'I can't help it,' Hayley panted as she came back down to earth with a series of tiny shudders that reverberated through her body. 'You make me feel so...so out of control.'

'You and me too, baby,' he said and a deep low groan burst from his throat as the waves of ecstasy washed over him.

'I love you,' she whispered as she stroked her fingers over his back. 'I love you.'

He didn't answer but she comforted herself as she listened to him drift off to sleep a few minutes later that he still had her in his arms, her head pressed to his chest over the steady beating of his heart.

CHAPTER SIXTEEN

HAYLEY WAS BOTH relieved and disappointed when she came downstairs the next morning to find Jasper had already left for work, the brief note he'd left informing her he'd taken Daniel to school on the way. She had been sick three times and her stomach was still revolting at the thought of food. She couldn't imagine how she would have explained it if either of them had seen or heard her stumbling about the bathroom as she showered and dressed for work.

Lucy winced when she saw Hayley's pale face as she came into the salon. 'Was it positive?'

Hayley nodded, doing her best not to cry.

'I don't know what to say,' Lucy said. 'I can't help feeling Jasper's going to let you down. His track record with pregnant girlfriends isn't great.'

'I'm his w-wife.' Hayley sniffed. 'Not his girlfriend.'

'I know, but for how long?'

'Not long enough.'

'He's a user, Hayley,' she said. 'You'll be better off without him.'

'He's not a user. He's a wonderful person. You don't know him as I do.'

'Yeah, well, try telling that to Mrs Beckforth,' Lucy said. 'She's booked in to see you at ten.'

Hayley felt her stomach tilt. 'Oh…'

'I was prepared to give Jasper a chance, but after what she told me when she phoned a few minutes ago I've decided he's up to no good,' Lucy said. 'God, Hayley, surely you can see it? He married you to get his hands on even more money, but he won't give a cent to the mother of his child for his upkeep. You're going to end up the same, or you will if you ever decide to tell him about your pregnancy.'

Hayley bit her lip. She wasn't sure she should reveal the content of her conversation with Jasper, even to her best friend.

'You're a fool, Hayley,' Lucy carried on. 'When he's finished with you he'll treat you the same way he's treated Miriam.'

'There are always two sides to these sorts of stories,' Hayley put in.

Lucy rolled her eyes. 'God, he really did a good job on you, didn't he? That lethal Caulfield charm has just claimed yet another victim.'

'You're wrong about him, Lucy,' she said. 'I just know you are.'

'That remains to be seen,' Lucy said.

The salon door chimed as someone entered and Hayley let out a sigh of relief as Lucy stepped from behind the counter to greet her first client of the day.

At ten a.m. on the dot the door chimed again and June Beckforth came into the salon, but instead of her usual slightly cloying smile she was snarling.

'Hello, Mrs Beckforth,' Hayley greeted her politely.

June's cold grey eyes insolently raked Hayley from head to foot. 'So you're his bit of fluff now, are you?' she asked with a curl of her thin lips. 'I thought you would have had more sense considering what I've told you about him.'

'I am Jasper's wife, if that's what you mean,' she said calmly, trying not to be intimidated by the venomous glare she was receiving.

June gave a laugh that sounded like water going down a partially blocked drain. 'You think you're so smart having married him, don't you? But it won't last, you know. I know all about Gerald's will. It was because of my son Martin that he changed it.'

Hayley frowned in confusion. 'What do you mean?'

'Martin told the old man the truth about Jasper. The dirty little secret Jasper would give anything to keep quiet.'

Hayley waited for her to continue, her heart beginning to thud behind the wall of her chest. What dirty little secret? What on earth did she mean?

'Jasper doesn't want Martin to tell the truth,' June continued. 'It would destroy too many lives, he said. But do you think we care about that now? He's been paying both of us to keep quiet, but I'm not going to keep quiet any more and neither is my son.'

'Paying you?' Hayley blinked at her in confusion. 'But I thought you said the last time I saw you that Jasper wouldn't provide for his son—for as long as I can remember you've always berated him for abandoning Miriam and Daniel financially.'

The older woman's expression looked triumphant. 'He hasn't told you, has he?' she asked.

'T-told me what?' Hayley's voice sounded whisper-thin. 'What hasn't he told me?'

'The dirty little secret he wants kept safe at all costs,' June said. 'Jasper isn't Daniel's father.'

Hayley's mouth dropped open, her heart feeling as if it had hit the floor and bounced right up again to lodge in the wrong position in her chest. She couldn't breathe properly; the air felt thick, like wet cotton wool as she tried to drag it into her lungs.

'So Jasper has always known he wasn't Daniel's father?' she asked when she could finally get her voice to work.

'Yes.'

'But I don't understand. Why didn't Miriam say so right from the start?'

'Because she had someone she wanted to protect—they both did. When Martin married her he found out the truth. He wouldn't have said anything except he's angry at what Jasper accused him of. And I support him one hundred per cent. No one's going to call my Martin a wife basher and get away with it.'

Hayley felt disgusted by the woman's attitude. How could she and her appalling excuse for a son have used Jasper in such a despicable way?

And yet Jasper had stood by the little boy caught in the middle.

Hayley took a steadying breath. 'So you and Martin are blackmailing Jasper.'

'You don't know that husband of yours very well if you think he can be blackmailed,' Miriam said. 'He drip-feeds us from time to time, but he's become a little cagey of late. He's made up some lies about Martin roughing up Daniel, but that boy needs a firm hand. The harder, the better, I say.'

Hayley felt like being sick. 'You *condone* such violence?'

June lifted one shoulder dismissively. 'He's a surly brat. He needs pulling into line occasionally. Martin has tried his best to get through to him but he won't budge. I told Miriam she should have had an abortion in the first place, then none of this would have happened, but apparently someone talked her out of it all those years ago.'

Hayley felt her belly clench painfully and her hand instinctively went down to press against it protectively. 'Do you know who it was?' she asked.

'Jasper, of course.'

Hayley felt such shame and regret flood her being she was barely able to stand up. For most of her young adult life she had judged Jasper so harshly, so unfairly, and yet he had been the one person to show some measure of integrity in a mess that had had no easy answer. He had thought about the child, the tiny, defenceless child caught up in it all, and had acted in Daniel's defence. Jasper had sacrificed his own reputation, his future and even his father's respect to give a small child a father to call his own.

'Who is Daniel's real father?' she asked.

'That's another thing I'm surprised you haven't guessed,' June said.

'But you're not going to tell me, are you?' Hayley said.

'I'm keeping that information up my sleeve as a bargaining tool.'

'I won't be blackmailed by you.'

June laughed her gurgling-drain laugh again. 'You're turning into a clone of that husband of yours,' she said. 'You're a fool, Hayley. He's using you just like he's used everybody else in his life. He wants Crickglades, not you.'

'I know that.'

June's eyebrows lifted. 'So you know he's going to divorce you as soon as he can?'

'I went into this marriage with my eyes wide open.'

'You love him, don't you?'

Hayley didn't bother confirming or denying it.

'I always knew there was something going on between you,' June said. 'Every time we talked about him I sensed it.'

'I love him,' Hayley said. 'He's a wonderful man who has been maligned for most of his life. I'm going to do my best to make it up to him.'

'He's going to break your heart,' June said. 'He's a player, not a stayer.'

'I'm prepared to risk it.'

'You've got your head in the clouds,' June said. 'Men like Jasper don't change.'

'I don't want him to change,' Hayley said. 'I love him just the way he is.'

June gave her a scathing look. 'He's not going to stand by you. He's always operated by his own code.'

'At least he has a moral code,' she said. 'How can you live with yourself? What sort of mother are you to encourage your son to exploit innocent people in such a way?'

'Martin's a good son,' she said. 'I warned him about marrying a single mother but he went ahead with it. He's tried to be a father to Daniel even though that kid resists all of his attempts to discipline him as any real father should.'

'What about Daniel?' Hayley asked. 'Does *he* know who his real father is?'

'No, and he's not going to like it when he finds out either,' June said.

Hayley felt ill with the thought of who it might be. What if Daniel's father was some sort of horrible person, a criminal of some sort—a murderer or rapist? Hadn't she felt the same horrible dread for most of her life? How would the poor boy cope with the stigma of knowing his veins carried criminal blood? No wonder Jasper had seemed so tense and on edge just lately. June had hinted the revelation would be a bombshell, but just how big a bombshell was anybody's guess.

'I'm going to have to ask you to leave,' Hayley said as the salon door opened.

June's face curled up in another sneer as she leaned closer so the client who had just come in wouldn't hear. 'Just remember what I said. And tell that husband of yours he's got a week before we go to the press and sell our story.'

Hayley gripped the edge of the counter so tightly she felt as if her fingers were going to break. She fought against the rising tide of nausea and took a couple of shallow breaths to steady herself.

Lucy came out just as June was leaving and, giving Hayley

a quick concerned glance, suggested she go and sit out the back for a while.

'I take it June Beckforth changed her mind about having the deluxe collagen facial,' she said once Hayley had dropped into the nearest chair.

'Yes, she apparently can't afford it at the moment,' Hayley said, feeling her colour drain even further.

'You don't have another booking until twelve. I'll keep an eye on the phone.'

'Thanks, Lucy,' she said and closing her office door, sat down and put her head in her hands.

Instead of going straight back to Jasper's house after work Hayley took a detour and called into Raymond's inner-city parish. He wasn't at his small house, but when she walked into the church she saw him lighting a candle near the altar.

He turned around at the sound of her footfall and came down and took both her hands in his. 'Hayley, what's wrong? You've been crying. Has Jasper upset you?'

She shook her head and choked back her sobs. 'No. I just felt the need to see you. I have so much on my mind. You said if ever I was in trouble you'd be there for me... Well...I'm in trouble.'

He led her to one of the pews and sat down beside her, his expression tender with concern. 'What's happened?'

'I'm pregnant.'

He paused for a moment. 'A child is a gift from God, Hayley.'

'I know...' Her sniff echoed loudly in the empty church. 'I want this baby so much but I can't tell Jasper.'

'But why ever not, my dear? He's your husband.'

She looked at him through tear-washed eyes. 'But you know what it's been like for him. It's made him bitter and yet I found out today it's not his fault.'

'What's not his fault?'

She took a moment to blow her nose. 'He's not Daniel's father,' she said, looking down at the scrunched-up tissues in her hand. 'Miriam's mother-in-law came to see me. She told me someone else is Daniel's father. She wouldn't say who. She and Martin Beckforth are using the information as a bribe to extort money out of Jasper. For all these years I've thought he was a neglectful father. I hated him for being selfish and yet he's the most unselfish person I've ever met. He's sacrificed so much for the sake of a child who he's known all along isn't his.'

There was another short silence.

'Does Daniel know who his father is?' Raymond asked.

'No…that's what's so terribly upsetting.' She turned to look at him again, blinking back tears. 'June Beckforth doesn't seem to care what effect it will have on Daniel to find out his father is some sort of creep or criminal.'

'Is that what she said?' He visibly paled with shock. 'That the boy's father is a criminal?'

'No…not really…' She chewed at her lip for a second. 'She just said it would be a bombshell revelation. She's even threatening to sell her story to the newspapers. I just assumed it must be someone disreputable otherwise why would Jasper want to keep it quiet for all this time? He's trying to protect Daniel.'

'No, he's not,' Raymond said heavily. 'He's not doing it to protect Daniel at all.'

'He's not?' Hayley blinked at him in puzzlement. 'Then who *is* he protecting?'

Raymond looked at her with deep sadness in his hazel eyes. 'He's doing it to protect me.'

'You?' She blinked at him again. 'Why would he be doing it to protect you? You're a priest, for God's…I mean, for Pete's sake. You deal with this sort of stuff all the time, you know people's confessions and—' She stopped when she saw the glimmer of tears sprout in his eyes, the sudden silence so heavy she could hear the faint flickering of the candles on the altar.

Raymond took a breath that sounded as if it hurt him deep inside and said, 'Jasper's doing it to protect me because I'm Daniel's father.'

CHAPTER SEVENTEEN

HAYLEY STARED AT him in a stunned silence.

Raymond got to his feet and sent a shaking hand through his thinning hair. 'For years I have tried to forget about the one time I betrayed my promise to God. I begged Him for forgiveness and moved on. I have felt the call for the priesthood since I was a young choirboy. I didn't want anything to stop me from achieving my goal of serving the community.' He turned to look at her, his expression tortured with guilt. 'I had no idea Daniel was mine. Not until this very moment. Like you I had assumed Jasper was responsible. Our father assumed it too. Everyone assumed it. And why shouldn't they? I had rarely strayed from the straight and narrow, certainly not with the frequency Jasper did. He was in and out of trouble all the time. I made one error, but I had no idea it would have these sorts of repercussions.'

'I don't know what to say… This must have come as a tremendous shock to you,' she said. 'I'm so sorry. I had no idea. I just wanted to talk to you about my own dilemma never once suspecting you were somehow connected to it.'

'For once in my life I don't have the answers, Hayley,' he said. 'I'm the one everyone comes to for help and guidance and yet I am at a loss to know what to do. And yet I can't help thinking of the boy. That poor young man has never known his real father.'

'I think June and Martin Beckforth are wrong,' Hayley said. 'They think Daniel will be disappointed by finding out who his real father is, but I don't agree. In fact, I can't help wondering if he already knows. He and Jasper are very close.'

He gave her an agonised glance. 'I have to come forward and claim him as mine. What will my parishioners think of me?'

Hayley got to her feet and gave his arm an affectionate squeeze. 'They'll think you're human, Raymond, just like the rest of us. No one is perfect and certainly not all the time. If God can forgive you, then I don't see why your parishioners can't do so as well.'

He smiled a sad smile. 'You're a wise young woman, Hayley. Jasper is a very lucky man.'

'For another few days,' she said with a droop to her mouth. 'He still wants our marriage to end.'

'Then I will keep praying for a miracle,' he said. 'Go home to him, Hayley, and tell him about his baby. God knows I wish I had been told all those years ago about mine.'

'Even though it might have meant you would have lost everything you held most dear?' she asked.

'I would have not lost as much as Jasper has done on my behalf,' he said. 'Our father believed the worst of him. He has been tainted with the shame of this for too long. He deserves to be free from it at last.'

'He and Miriam did what they thought was best at the time,' she said. 'Jasper knew how devoted you were to your faith. He wouldn't let anything stand in the way of your dreams.'

Raymond gave another deep regretful sigh. 'And yet I have inadvertently stood in the way of his…'

* * *

Hayley came into the lounge an hour later to find Jasper pacing the room, his face like carved stone as he swung to face her. 'Where the hell have you been?' he barked at her furiously.

'I was visiting Raymond. I wanted to—'

'Would you care to explain to me the meaning of this?' He thrust the crumpled pregnancy-testing kit package at her.

She froze as she looked at it. 'Where did you find it?'

'*I* didn't find it,' he bit out. 'Rosario came dancing down the stairs with it in absolute raptures, congratulating me effusively. I can only assume from her reaction that the test you conducted turned out to be positive.'

She swallowed. 'Yes…yes, it did…'

'I've taken the liberty of packing your things for you,' he said coldly. 'I've already sent Eric around to your flat with them. I will be serving divorce papers on you as soon as possible.'

Hayley couldn't seem to locate her voice. She could hardly believe what she was hearing. Shock and pain had turned her stomach into a churning pit of despair. She was frightened she was going to be sick or even faint. Her fingertips felt icy as the blood drained away from her extremities to thud through her brain with skull-cracking force.

'You warned me you were going to make me regret marrying you, didn't you?' he said. 'But little did I think the way you would do it was to foist another man's child on me. The irony, if only you knew, is particularly astounding. But I'm not coming to the party. I want you out of here and if I ever see you again it will be a minute too soon.'

'Jasper…' she managed to choke out 'you surely don't think I would—'

'I'm not hanging around here to listen to your pathetic attempts to weasel your way out of this,' he cut her off. 'Now I know why you so readily agreed to marry me instead of Lederman—you thought I was the bigger fish to land. No doubt you're going to run away with him now on the spoils of your divorce from me. I heard him mention something about a baby when you met him in the bar that night. You must have cooked this up between you all along. He fathered your child while I've been primed to pay for it.'

'I can't believe you're—'

'That was a nice touch telling me you loved me,' he went on bitterly. 'You nearly had me fooled which shows just how hard-nosed you've turned out to be. But you forget I've seen it all before. I'm no stranger to the manipulative wiles of women who have dollar signs for eyeballs.'

Hayley was perilously close to tears but her pride insisted she hold back until she was alone. She needed time to think without this bombardment of shattered emotions disrupting her brain. So much had happened in such a short time she felt totally shell-shocked. Jasper, too, needed time to let the dust settle. He hadn't given her a chance to tell him what she'd stumbled upon this evening, but all she could hope was that when he did hear of it, it would make him rethink some of his assumptions about her.

She watched in desolation as he left the room without a backward glance. She let out the tight breath she'd been holding and, tugging off her engagement and wedding ring, left them on the coffee-table near the sofa.

Then, with her heart breaking, she picked up her bag and keys and walked out of his life.

Three months later…

'Your next client is here,' Lucy said as she poked her head around the waxing-room door.

Hayley glanced at the clock on the wall. 'But I don't have

another client until three. I checked the book just before Mrs Pritchard came in for her eyebrow and lash tint.'

'It was a last-minute thing,' Lucy said. 'It's a young guy with troubled skin. I think he just needs a deep cleanse or an express facial or something. I would have done it but he asked for you.'

Hayley came out to Reception to see Daniel Moorebank sitting on the edge of one of the chairs. He stood up and smiled shyly. 'Hello, Hayley.'

'Hi, Daniel,' she answered. 'How are you?'

'I'm fine. Great, actually…er…except for my skin, of course.'

As far as she could tell there was absolutely nothing wrong with his skin. 'What can I do for you?' she asked.

He flushed and pointed to a small, almost invisible blemish on one cheek. 'I was wondering if you could help me clear this up. Can we…er…talk in private?'

'Of course,' she said. 'Come into the treatment room.'

She waited until he was seated in the consultation chair before she inspected his face. 'You've got great skin, Daniel.'

He flushed again, reminding her so much of his father she felt a sudden tightening in her chest. Raymond had told her of his first official meeting with his son, how it had gone, and how poignant it had been. Hayley's hunch had been right: Daniel had already suspected who his father was but had forbidden Jasper to reveal the truth for the sake of Raymond's position in the community. But in the end Raymond had decided to leave the priesthood and pursue a career in social work, which had already brought both him and Daniel a great deal of happiness.

Hayley hadn't heard from Jasper. She had sent him rent money but the envelopes had been returned each time unopened. She wasn't sure what to make of that but assumed he was determined to cut off all contact, even though he owned the property she lived in.

She had seen a photo of him in one of the gossip magazines;

he had been surrounded by group of glamorous young women, which seemed to indicate he had well and truly moved on.

'So…how are you?' Daniel asked, his hazel eyes slipping briefly to the slight bulge of her abdomen.

'I'm fine,' she said. 'I'm over the worst of the morning sickness now.'

'That's good.'

There was an awkward silence.

Hayley watched as Daniel fidgeted in his chair, his eyes flicking anywhere but to hers.

'He loves you,' he suddenly announced baldly, meeting her eyes at last. 'He really loves you.'

'Who?'

Daniel rolled his eyes. 'Jasper, of course.'

Hayley tightened her mouth. 'Then why doesn't he come in here and tell me himself?'

'He's too proud,' he said. 'I keep telling him he's got to get himself sorted out but he won't listen. I'm worried about him.'

'I'm sure he'll find someone else to console himself with,' she said. 'Or several someones.'

'No,' Daniel insisted. 'You don't understand. He's totally screwed up over this. He doesn't want a divorce, I know he doesn't.'

'He has a funny way of showing it,' she remarked wryly.

'He thought you were going to rip him off, but you didn't ask for a thing. You even left the rings he bought you behind. He wasn't expecting that.'

'How do you think I've felt for the last three months vomiting every time I think of food with no one to support me?' she said.

Daniel looked uncomfortable. 'I know it must have been tough, but he's a bit stubborn, as you know.' He reached into the back pocket of his jeans, took out a piece of computer paper and handed it to her. 'You should read this before you give up on him. I saw it by accident when I was doing an assignment on his computer. It's an email from his lawyer documenting that the flat you're living in is now yours.'

Hayley stared at the message, hardly able to believe her eyes. It was there in black and white, the flat was now in her name.

'Will you at least come and see him?' Daniel asked into the long silence. 'He's been so wonderful to me. He's set up a trust fund for me so I can go to agricultural college in a couple of years' time. The property he bought in the Southern Highlands is for me. It's what I've always dreamed of doing. I can't believe he's been so generous. He's waiting on council approval on Crickglades to come through, but when it does he's going to incorporate a big youth centre complex there. He's getting the gardens his mother designed restored so they can be enjoyed by everyone who visits.

'I've been staying with him on and off for the last three months but it's not the same without you there. Rosario says the same. I know the spelling's different but you're like Halley's comet. You're the only bright thing he's had in his life in years.'

She pursed her mouth at him. 'You know, I can tell you're a Caulfield,' she said. 'You're already showing signs of that lethal charm.'

He smiled. 'I don't know how to thank you for what you did for me in uncovering the truth before my mother's husband could go to the press. I have two fathers now instead of one. Raymond is a great guy. I can't believe the way he has given up everything to be there for me. But then I think of Jasper and he's the same. The greatest love a person can show for another is to give their life for another person. Jasper did that for me when I needed it most.'

Hayley struggled to hold the tears back. 'Will he be home this evening?'

'I'll make sure he is,' he said. 'I'll make myself scarce so you can talk to him in private.'

'You don't have to do that; it's your home as well.'

'Not for much longer. I'm going back to Mum's now that creep has moved out since she told him she wants a divorce. But in the meantime I'm going to spend more and more time at Raymond's place. He and I have some stuff planned with some homeless kids. I'm helping him with a community project. I love it. It's so amazing seeing the change in young kids' lives.'

Tears sprang from her eyes. 'Daniel, I'm so proud of you,' she said. 'You really are one special guy.'

He grinned at her as he got to his feet. 'So you think my skin's OK, then, do you?'

She stepped up on tiptoe and kissed his cheek. 'Everything about you is perfect, Daniel.'

Hayley took a deep breath as she stood in front of the intercom panel outside Jasper's house. She decided against pressing it and used the code instead. She still had a key to his house and approached the front door with it shaking slightly in her hand.

She opened the door and listened for sounds of movement but all was silent. She stepped inside, her ears still straining, but there was no indication anyone was at home.

Disappointment surged through her. She had been building herself up to this for the whole afternoon. It didn't seem fair that no one was here to receive her.

She sat on one of the sofas, her spirits sagging as she wondered if Daniel had got it wrong. Jasper might be out with a new lover, or even worse bring someone back with him.

She jerked upright when she heard the roar of his car nosing its way into the garage. She waited with bated breath for the sound of his footsteps, her legs wobbling as she got to her feet as he came into the room.

His eyes widened in shock when he saw her, his face visibly draining of colour. 'What are you doing here?' he asked.

'I wanted to see you.'

'What about?'

She tried not to be put off by his curt and too rapid response. 'I thought you might like an update on your child's progress,' she said.

His gaze flicked to her swollen abdomen before returning to hers. 'You seem pretty sure it is mine, but I'd like confirmation first.'

'That can easily be arranged.'

'So you'll agree to it?' he asked.

'I have no reason not to.'

Her response had obviously not been the one he'd been expecting. She could see the flicker of uncertainty in his dark eyes. 'What's happened to Lederman?' he asked.

'Last thing I heard he was sailing off into the sunset with a buxom blonde with a fortune in stocks and shares,' she said.

'So he's left you in the lurch.'

'No,' she said. 'You have.'

'What do you mean by that?'

'I'm having your baby.'

'You expect me to believe that?'

'Yes as a matter of fact I do.'

'Why are you here?' he asked.

'Because Daniel told me you loved me.'

'And you believed him?'

'He's a nice kid,' she said. 'He doesn't have any reason to lie.'

'But you do.'

'I have never lied to you, Jasper. I told you I loved you and I meant it. I'm having your baby even if you don't want to acknowledge it as yours.'

He looked at her, his eyes growing darker by the second,

the glisten of moisture unmistakable. 'Is it really my baby?' he asked, his voice cracking over the words.

Hayley started to cry as she stumbled towards him. 'Of course it is, you big, dumb, gorgeous, arrogant fool. How could you possibly think I would ever look at anyone but you?'

He buried his head into the fragrance of her springy hair, pulling her tightly into his body. 'I never realised until I saw that pregnancy test how much I wanted it to be mine. I had told myself for years I wouldn't put my hand up again to claim someone else's child, having seen the damage it does when secrets come out when and where they shouldn't.'

'It must have been so hard for you,' she said. 'There was so much pressure on you. Everyone blamed you, including me.'

'I was OK about supporting Daniel even though I always knew I wasn't his father,' he said. 'Miriam came to me and asked for my advice. I offered to do what I could to support her. I hadn't factored in my father's reaction. He demanded that I marry her, but she and I both knew that wasn't an option. I couldn't stand by and watch everything my brother had longed for taken away because of one mistake. I decided it would be the best thing all round if I accepted the blame. And to tell you the truth I have never once regretted it until Martin Beckforth came on the scene and started throwing his weight around. Then I wondered if I had done the right thing after all, but Daniel assures me he's thrilled with how things have turned out. Miriam's finally getting a divorce, which is a huge relief to him.'

'Daniel is as much your son as he is Raymond's,' she said, looking up at him. 'You have been the most amazing father to him, as you will be to our child.'

'So you're willing to take a risk on me?' he asked. 'To stay married to me and bring up our baby together?'

She smiled up at him rapturously. 'As far as I'm concerned there's no risk involved, darling.' She placed his hand on her belly where his child was already tentatively starting to stretch its limbs. 'I'm not going to stop loving you, not after all this time.'

'I love you too,' Jasper said, his voice so deep and raw it hurt his throat. 'I'm not sure when I started loving you. It's sort of crept up on me. The last three months have proven that if nothing else.'

'Why didn't you contact me?'

'I picked up the phone so many times but my pride got in the way. I kept telling myself you were going back to Lederman and I was better off without you. Daniel made me realise how dumb I was being. He said I was a fool to let someone like you slip through my fingers.'

'So we're really not getting divorced?' she asked as she pressed closer to his hardening warmth.

'What do you think, baby girl?' he said with a slow, sexy smile. 'Do you fancy being married to me for longer?'

'What sort of time frame were you thinking of this time around?'

He brought his mouth within a breath of her smiling one. 'How about for ever?'

Hayley gazed dreamily at the sensual curve of his mouth. 'Starting from when?' she asked in a breathy whisper.

'Starting from now,' he said, and captured her sigh of joy with the heat of his kiss.

HARLEQUIN *Presents*

Enjoy two exciting,
festive stories to put you
in a holiday mood!

THE BOSS'S CHRISTMAS BABY
by Trish Morey
Book #2678

Tegan Fielding is supposed to be masquerading for
her twin, not sleeping with her sister's boss! But how
will sexy James Maverick react when he discovers his
convenient mistress is expecting the boss's baby?

JED HUNTER'S RELUCTANT BRIDE
by Susanne James
Book #2682

It's Christmastime when wealthy Jed Hunter offers
Cryssie a job, and she's forced to take it. Soon Jed
demands Cryssie marry him—it makes good business
sense. But Cryssie's feelings run deeper....

Available November wherever you buy books.

www.eHarlequin.com

HPCM1107

THE ROYAL HOUSE OF NIROLI

Always passionate, always proud.

**The richest royal family in the world—
a family united by blood and passion,
torn apart by deceit and desire.**

By royal decree, Harlequin Presents is delighted to bring you
THE ROYAL HOUSE OF NIROLI. Step into the glamorous,
enticing world of the Nirolian royal family. As the king ails,
he must find an heir. Each month an exciting new installment
follows the epic search for the true Nirolian king.

Eight heirs, eight romances, eight fantastic stories!

Available November

EXPECTING HIS ROYAL BABY

by Susan Stephens

Book #2675

Carrie has been in love with Nico Fierezza for years. After
one night of loving, he discarded her...now she's carrying
his child! Carrie will do anything to protect the future of
her baby—including marrying Nico?

Be sure not to miss any of the passion!

Coming in December:
THE PRINCE'S FORBIDDEN VIRGIN by Robyn Donald
Book#2683

www.eHarlequin.com

HP12675

REQUEST YOUR FREE BOOKS!

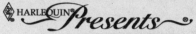 HARLEQUIN® *Presents* ®

2 FREE NOVELS PLUS 2
FREE GIFTS!

YES! Please send me 2 FREE Harlequin Presents® novels and my 2 FREE gifts. After receiving them, if I don't wish to receive any more books, I can return the shipping statement marked "cancel." If I don't cancel, I will receive 6 brand-new novels every month and be billed just $3.80 per book in the U.S., or $4.47 per book in Canada, plus 25¢ shipping and handling per book and applicable taxes, if any*. That's a savings of close to 15% off the cover price! I understand that accepting the 2 free books and gifts places me under no obligation to buy anything. I can always return a shipment and cancel at any time. Even if I never buy another book from Harlequin, the two free books and gifts are mine to keep forever.

106 HDN EEXK   306 HDN EEXV

Name	(PLEASE PRINT)	
Address		Apt. #
City	State/Prov.	Zip/Postal Code

Signature (if under 18, a parent or guardian must sign)

Mail to the **Harlequin Reader Service®**:
IN U.S.A.: P.O. Box 1867, Buffalo, NY 14240-1867
IN CANADA: P.O. Box 609, Fort Erie, Ontario L2A 5X3

Not valid to current Harlequin Presents subscribers.

Want to try two free books from another line?
Call 1-800-873-8635 or visit www.morefreebooks.com.

* Terms and prices subject to change without notice. NY residents add applicable sales tax. Canadian residents will be charged applicable provincial taxes and GST. This offer is limited to one order per household. All orders subject to approval. Credit or debit balances in a customer's account(s) may be offset by any other outstanding balance owed by or to the customer. Please allow 4 to 6 weeks for delivery.

Your Privacy: Harlequin is committed to protecting your privacy. Our Privacy Policy is available online at www.eHarlequin.com or upon request from the Reader Service. From time to time we make our lists of customers available to reputable firms who may have a product or service of interest to you. If you would prefer we not share your name and address, please check here. ☐

HP07

HARLEQUIN *Presents*

INNOCENT MISTRESS, VIRGIN WIFE

Wedded and bedded for the very first time

Classic romances from
your favorite Presents authors

Available this month:

THE SPANISH DUKE'S VIRGIN BRIDE
by Chantelle Shaw
#2679

Ruthless billionaire Duke Javier Herrera needs a wife
to inherit the family business. Grace is the daughter
of a man who's conned Javier, and in this he sees an
opportunity for revenge and a convenient wife....

Coming soon,
THE DEMETRIOS BRIDAL BARGAIN
by Kim Lawrence
Book #2686

www.eHarlequin.com

HP12679

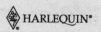

Mediterranean NIGHTS™

*Not everything is above board
on Alexandra's Dream!*

*Enjoy plenty of secrets, drama and sensuality
in the latest from Mediterranean Nights.*

Coming in November 2007...

BELOW DECK

by

Dorien Kelly

Determined to protect her young son,
widow Mei Lin Wang keeps him hidden
aboard *Alexandra's Dream* under cover of
her job. But life gets extremely complicated
when the ship's security officer, Gideon Dayan,
is piqued by the mystery surrounding this
beautiful, haunted woman....

www.eHarlequin.com   HM38965

Men who can't be tamed...or so they think!

If you love strong, commanding men,
you'll love this brand-new miniseries.

Meet the guy who breaks the rules to get exactly
what he wants, because he is...

HARD-EDGED & HANDSOME

He's the man who's impossible to resist....

RICH & RAKISH

He's got everything—and needs nobody...
until he meets one woman....

He's RUTHLESS!

In his pursuit of passion; in his world the winner takes all!

Coming in November:

THE BILLIONAIRE'S CAPTIVE BRIDE

by Emma Darcy
Book #2676

Coming in December:

BEDDED, OR WEDDED?

by Julia James
Book #2684

Brought to you by your favorite Harlequin Presents authors!

www.eHarlequin.com

HP12676

I ♥ HARLEQUIN® *Presents*

BROUGHT TO YOU BY FANS OF
HARLEQUIN PRESENTS.

We are its editors and authors
and biggest fans—and we'd
love to hear from YOU!

Subscribe today to our online blog at
www.iheartpresents.com

HPBLOG